James A. Levine, a Professor of Medicine at the Mayo Clinic, is a world renowned scientist, doctor, and researcher. For his scientific work, Dr. Levine has regularly appeared on CNN, the BBC, the CBC, and the Discovery Channel. He lives in Oronoco, Minnesota.

THE BLUE NOTEBOOK

Batuk is a fifteen-year-old girl from rural India. When she was recovering from TB in hospital she learned to read. Her only possessions are a pencil and a blue notebook in which she writes her journal . . . She records that her father sold her into sexual slavery when she was nine. And how, as she navigates the grim realities of the Common Street — a street of prostitution in Mumbai where children are kept in cages as they wait for customers — she manages to put pen to paper. Her private thoughts and stories are all put down. Through the words that Batuk writes in her journal, she finds hope and beauty in the bleakest of situations.

JAMES A. LEVINE

◆

THE BLUE NOTEBOOK

Complete and Unabridged

06200652

ULVERSCROFT
Leicester

First published in Great Britain in 2009 by
Weidenfeld & Nicolson
An imprint of
The Orion Publishing Group Ltd., London

First Large Print Edition
published 2010
by arrangement with
The Orion Publishing Group Ltd.
An Hachette UK Company, London

The moral right of the author has been asserted

British Library CIP Data

Levine, James, *1963 –*
The blue notebook.
1. Teenage girls- -India- -Bombay- -Fiction.
2. Teenage prostitution- -India- -Bombay- -Fiction.
3. Diaries- -Authorship- -Fiction. 4. Bombay (India)- -
Social conditions- -Fiction. 5. Large type books.
I. Title
813.6–dc22

ISBN 978–1–44480–022–7

Published by
F. A. Thorpe (Publishing)
Anstey, Leicestershire

Set by Words & Graphics Ltd.
Anstey, Leicestershire
Printed and bound in Great Britain by
T. J. International Ltd., Padstow, Cornwall

This book is printed on acid-free paper

For my daughters

I am grateful to Celina Spiegel and Natanya Wheeler.

This book would not have been possible without the help and support of the following: The Food and Agricultural Organization of the United Nations, the World India Diabetes Foundation, the Indian Police, the National and International Centers for Missing and Exploited Children and Dr. Michael Tomlinson, and my friends and colleagues across the scientific community. Without the encouragement of my family, friends, and children, in particular, I would not have written this book.

Most of all, without Batuk, the girl in the pink sari with the rainbow trim, there would be no story to tell.

James Levine
Prague
October 7, 2007

A portion of the proceeds of *The Blue Notebook* is being donated to the International

Center for Missing and Exploited Children (www.icmec.org) and the National Center for Missing and Exploited Children: (www.missingkids.com). For more information, visit www.BatukFoundation.org.

The blue notebook

I have a break now. Mamaki Briila is pleased with me and she should be! I have worked hard all morning and now that I tell her I am tired, she smiles at me. 'Rest, little Batuk,' she says. 'Today will be brimming with riches.' Actually, I am not tired at all.

My name is Batuk. I am a fifteen-year-old girl nested in the Common Street in Mumbai. I have been here six years and I have been blessed with beauty and a pencil. My beauty comes from within. The pencil came from the ear of Mamaki Briila, who is my boss.

I saw the pencil fall from Mamaki's ear two nights ago. I had just made sweet-cake and she bustled into my nest with an immense smile, leaned over, pinched my cheek, and kissed the top of my head. As she bent over, the giant sacs of her breasts were thrown in my face so that I could actually see the sparkling of sweat between them. She smelled like us, but worse.

She had to hold her back and lurch to get

1

upright again, and as she did her breasts swayed as if they were pets hanging from her neck, dancing. She pulled the pencil from behind her ear and withdrew a palm-sized yellow notebook from an inner fold of her sari (or maybe her skin). As she opened the book, she peered down at me and another smile spread over her red face like water soaking into dry stone. She made a pencil mark in her book with a flourish of her bloated hand. She said sweetly, 'Little Batuk, you are my favorite girl. I thought you were going to disappoint me tonight but in just an hour, you have made me love you.' I am sure she was about to remind me of her thousand kindnesses to me but she was interrupted by a shriek from Puneet.

Puneet is my best friend and occupies the nest two down from me. Puneet rarely cries, unlike Princess Meera, who cries every time she makes sweet-cake. Puneet only cries when he has to and the shriek he emitted that moment could have split rock. It was a single piercing yell, not of bodily pain, because Puneet feels no pain, but of terror. Mamaki knew this too. Puneet is the most valuable of us all because he is a boy.

Puneet's scream killed the night silence of the street and the smile dropped from Mamaki's face like a coin falling to the ground. She turned her street-wide rear in my face and fled from my nest. I was impressed that an object set on earth as she is can move with such speed, when it has to. As she flew from my nest, the tails of her sari caught the breeze and reminded me of the sheets used to protect the crops from the summer sun. That is when the pencil slipped from behind Mamaki's ear, lubricated by her unique brand of body oil.

In Mamaki's wake, the pencil dropped to the floor of my nest, bounced a couple of times, and then stopped moving. I sprang from my bed and threw myself upon it. The pencil was mine by divine decree.

I lay upon the small object, silent and motionless. My mind went back to when I was a little girl in Dreepah-Jil, my home village. I would perch on a rock in the sun, sometimes for hours, even in the heat of midday, and imagine myself melting into the rock. Eventually from between the rocks or through the grass would scamper a little lizard. With its quick tight movements, it would look around and see nothing moving and feel safe. The lizard would relax and sun itself below my rock or sometimes even on it. I would not move, even if it sat right next to me. I would control my breathing and melt deeper into the rock until I became stone. I used my mind to control the mind of the lizard. I would speak soothingly to the lizard through the upper air. 'Relax, little lizard, you will soon be mine.'

You can look upward and see a raindrop that is destined to hit you. You see it, you know it is falling ever faster, and you know it will hit you, but you cannot escape it. So it was for the lizard. As I sprang upon the lizard, we might lock eyes for a hair of a moment. Then I would land on it, sometimes with so much force that I would kill it; if so, such was its fate. As I lay on the stone floor of my nest, I had a pencil because that too was fate.

I got off the floor, climbed onto my throne, lay down with the pencil under my belly, and fell asleep. When I awoke in the morning, the pencil was where I had left it but it had become warmed by my dreams. I lay in the first light with my eyes fluttering awake and asleep as I gazed through the entrance to my nest. I knew that there was not enough of this little pencil to write away my life, but there was enough to start.

My break and my faked tiredness are nearly over. In a moment I will replace this writing book inside the rip I made in my mattress. Today as I lie making sweet-cake, I will feel it against my back and know that it is there.

You should have heard Mamaki that night when she ran into Puneet's nest at the speed of gunfire. Her scream was almost as loud as Puneet's had been. His had been an expression of terror whereas hers was meant to generate it. There had been two servants paying homage together to Prince Puneet when the commotion erupted, a practice that is entirely acceptable to Mamaki if the gifts to the prince are correctly apportioned. In this case, the gifts were of less importance as the devotees were two high-ranking police officers. Although they had initially undertaken the acts of baking (I heard Mamaki bless the visitors when they arrived), things got out of hand. Puneet was ripped apart by a police stick.

Mamaki threw the officers into the Common Street with one massive shove. Pah! to the officers. As I watched them from my nest, they got up, brushed the dust off their tan uniforms, laughed like brothers, and ambled away into the night. One of them had his police stick dangling from his wrist. Puneet fell to the ground from it — drip, drip, drip — as if the earth needed to feed on Puneet just as they had done.

Forgive me, please, for I am being

dramatic. This is not only because Puneet is my beloved but also because I have a sense of drama. Mother always scolded me for this, perhaps because my playacting delighted Father so. When the family was together I would put on shows. I would mimic Navrang, the village lunatic, or Uncle Vishal ('Uncle V'), who was so fat he fell asleep in his soup. Mother would shake her head in grumbling disapproval whereas Father would laugh until he cried. I have always had a talent for such things.

As a reward for my drama, Father would take me into his arms and, if I begged him, he would tell me the story of the silver-eyed leopard. Every rendition had different embel-lishments and the story could last for hours, depending on how tired Father was or whether I fell asleep.

I loved my story. On some nights, I would pretend to be asleep when Mother walked through the bedroom filled with my brothers, sisters, and cousins. If I was still awake when Father returned from the fields and from the woman with the lavender scent, I would rush to him, fold myself in his lap, and beg him to tell me my story. 'Not tonight, Batuk,' he would often say as I cuddled into him and felt the vibration in his chest as he spoke. Twenty minutes or so later, as he brushed the last rice off his mouth, he would invariably give in and start telling me the story to my whoops of delight. You see, I was always Father's silver-eyed leopard.

★ ★ ★

Puneet has been ill but Mamaki says he is recovering. Between baking classes, I call to him two nests down and he calls back. Initially, Hippopotamus (this is how we secretly refer to Mamaki) forbade our volleys of chatter during work hours, but soon she realized that it lifts Puneet's spirits and now allows it.

Puneet is not yet ready to bake with us. If Puneet is so injured that he cannot work with us, or if he dies, then who will be there for me? I suppose that is a selfish way of thinking, but such is the whim of the dramatic soul.

~

There is a short break. Mr. Floppy Ears baked only the smallest sweet-cake with me. I can hardly claim to be tired.

I write in pencil. So how do I sharpen it, you ask? I smile at you. Not my 'come and adore me' smile but a sly smile. I sharpen my pencil with the quickness of my wits.

Two streets down from my nest is the Street of Thieves. Here you can buy everything from an airplane to a cloak that makes you invisible — or that's what they say. One of the barrow boys who carts goods to and from the Street of Thieves I call Bandu. Bandu the barrow boy passes in front of my nest at least twice a day. I know when he is coming because the barrow's wheel is steel and it makes a terrible racket, which I can hear from streets away. In the early morning, when he passes by, his barrow brims over with bits and pieces, and in the evening when he returns, the wooden box is almost empty. There are occasions too when he makes extra trips, presumably for special deliveries.

Bandu is about my age and fine to look at. Even over the last year he has become more masculine and taller. He has large oval eyes that stare at me every day and, without fail, stare away whenever I catch his gaze. I think he sleeps with me in his mind from time to time.

As my pencil became blunt I, the sly girl that I am, started smiling more avidly at him. I would tilt my head and show my lips. As I ensnared him to my will — like the lizard — his stare would linger and sometimes he would hold my gaze for a full second. On occasion, his eyes flicked, like the lizard's tongue, to my thighs or my small breasts. I sat in my nest as I had sat on my rock many years earlier, waiting for the barrow boy to sun himself under my shadow. He began to slow down as he approached my nest, and a few days later he grunted at me in that primal way shy men do.

After three days of grunting and my feigned embarrassment, I beckoned him to me. My gate's lock does not drop until after Hippo's first morning tea and cake, but I lowered my head below his, looked at him through my locked gate, and said, 'My name is Batuk. I desperately need your help.' I paused and smiled. 'You could get me a sharpener for my pencil.'

I was a little annoyed that he took a full two days to bring the sharpener to me. But when he did return, late, after Hippo's third tea, with it clasped in his street-worn hand, I smiled as if he had brought me a ruby. I then kissed him. There was no gate between us. I had intended to peck him on the cheek because I felt that was all he deserved, but instead I kissed him straight on the mouth. I searched my tongue for his and felt his tongue flee to the back of his mouth like a cowering dog about to be beaten. He started to push his tongue forward to meet mine, but I thrust him away with both my arms. This whole exchange of thanks took less than a few seconds but I knew that my taste would linger in his mouth all day. His want of me would soak his mind for far longer than that.

I do not know why I behaved in such a disgraceful manner, but I have my pencil sharpener and I never spoke to or acknowledged Bandu the barrow boy again.

~

The doctor came again yesterday to see Puneet and left after only ten minutes. This is probably because of the stench of Mamaki at close quarters and because Mamaki only pays a quarter of the doctor's fee. This doctor comes here frequently, though, Princess Meera being his first choice when it comes to topping off his bill.

The news from the doctor was good. It is only four days after Puneet's visit from the policemen and he is free from danger. I knew that I was being overdramatic! On a break, I leaned out of the entrance of my nest and called to Puneet, as I have been doing constantly, knowing that he is not working. He called back to say that he feels his strength returning. He did not want to say that he feels good because I know he fears the ears of Hippopotamus and wants to stretch out his recovery as long as possible.

Puneet will soon mature to manhood and I can see this in his body. His shoulders are becoming defined and his muscles more obvious. His thighs are bulging more and there are a few hairs on his shiny chest. His voice occasionally crackles. Although we have laughed about this we both know what it means. Soon a decision will need to be made about Puneet and he will not be the one to make it.

If Puneet is to lose his bhunnas they will need to do it soon (I thought that while the doctor was here, they would go right ahead and do it). If he is allowed to enter manhood, they will need to train his bhunnas and give him a new style. It is possible that as a man he may become more beautiful but there is also a chance he would become ugly and in that case he would need to be discarded. My vote would be to remove his bhunnas now. He will then always be as beautiful as he is today and he will always be there for me. There is no one who can make me laugh as hard as Puneet.

Regardless of what transpires, Puneet's eyes will be constant. I have looked into his eyes and there I see his laughter and his mockery of the nest, Hippopotamus, and the Common Street. As I stare deeper into him, I watch his disdain for those who adore him and a red splash of evil. Deeper still, I see a bottomless well of cool water that is love.

~

My nest is a womb of gold.

Picture me illuminated in white light. This light, if you could put some in a bottle and examine it, is composed of a dervish of all color but also of laughter and joy. As you hold the bottle and peer at it, your hand is warmed and you feel my grace. Should you open the bottle and be nimble enough to pour its contents into your mouth, you will never hunger again but instead catch fire — and so be light too. From my face emanate rivers of brilliance that seek out all specks of darkness, and this is how I light my nest. My nest is glowing in my light, for there is no other light.

My nest, as I call it, is my throne room. For all the many ravines and indentations within its interior, its external shape is simple — a rectangle. Stone, and a blue gate; that is all.

As I contemplate my physical surroundings, I can never reconcile how Father allowed me to come here. For all his tales, for all his wild laughter (where he would throw his head so far back I sometimes thought it would fall off), and for all his self-assurance that a bountiful destiny was mine, how could he let his silver-eyed leopard land here, laid upon this sacrificial altar?

That is unimportant for now. Look carefully at the walls of my throne room and you will see gold leaf hammered over every inch of brick. Where there was once gray brick, the foundation of the Common Street, here all you see is gold sparkling and winking at you in my bright light. Moreover, if you look carefully at the gold on the walls you will see the most intricate carvings. The craftsmen have depicted my life in its every detail. Look! There to my right are carvings of my cousins and sisters and strong brothers (except for Navaj, who is a year older than me and who was handicapped at birth). Look! There on the left toward the ceiling you see my family seated in the robes of the Spring Festivities. Look up on the roof — there! I am carved swimming at the river's bank, a naked unashamed six-year-old, and look, there is Grandpa, whom I barely remember (my goodness, he looks so thin). Around me, beaten and etched in the gold of my walls, is my likeness. The intricacy of the craftsmanship stands equal to the intricacies of my life, except there is no carving of slavery.

Against the innermost wall of my rectangular nest is my throne. The dim-witted say that I should have a throne of gold with pearl inlay and legs of ivory, and they ask why I chose instead the simple wood of the daruka tree to sit upon. This wood is said to be a thousand years old and has seen cities built and destroyed. The wood whispers the tales of warriors, of the great teachers and princes — you only have to ask it. Daruka wood may be strong and dense, but remember that it can be destroyed by a single match, just as a life of a thousand happenings and a million memories can be extinguished in a second.

Carved behind my throne in purest ivory is a silver-eyed leopard. Its white coat is speckled with diamond dust. The leopard's eyes shine like polished silver coins.

Man comes here to worship from every kingdom, and from my throne I cast dominion over my subjects. You cross my threshold and I welcome you at the gate, but ultimately it is my throne you seek to lie upon.

Simple as my throne may be, magnificent are its adornments. Its long cushions are filled with the under-feathers of a hundred fledgling eagles, which carry the young's flight of innocence. The feathers were collected from far-off lands, the names of which I do not even know. The cushions are encased in the hand-weaving of the youngest Kashmiri children, who performed this act of servitude with smiles and laughter, for they knew that upon their hands' work I will lie. The sunshine they work in is captured in the essence of the weave; the cushions are the orange-yellow of the last light of day. Woven into the cushions are patterns sewn with thread dyed in the blue blood of a secret sea creature; their ancient shapes convey mathematical and mystical meaning for those who understand them. I do not understand because I am a simple baker of sweet-cake.

You see, I lie on a bed of everlasting youth, and those who lie with me taste youth. It is not a bed of eternal life, for my life will only be eternal when I die.

Sometimes I pretend that I am deranged; it simply comes out of me. When I was a child, Mother would often harshly scold me for the tiniest of sins. 'Did you steal your brother's milk?' 'Why did you not clean as I told you?' 'Where is that sash you borrowed from your sister?' I would love to just stare at her as she screamed at me. I would look up into her eyes, look beyond her eyeballs, and stare into the emptiness that I knew left Father lonely. My eye-locked silence enraged her even more. She would then turn up the scream volume, increase the speed of spit coming from her mouth, deepen her breathing, sweat a little bit more, and, before me, become more putrid. All because I saw her for what she was.

Mother would often swipe me because my resilience was too great. Her red palm would slap my face with such vehemence that I felt she might break my neck. Before I howled in pain at these quite frequent assaults, I would try to hold back my scream because I wanted to build up my ability to reside within myself. Nowadays the strikes are not with the open henna-reddened hand of Mother but from the pounding of man's hips on mine. Mother trained me well, though, for now I do live within myself.

No! I am not deranged. I do not believe for a second that I lie each day in a nest of gold with attendants and creamy foods. My cell, with its steel bars, is the size of a toilet. That is my home. I wait for the gray concrete night to become day — not that it matters a speck, for the walls never change. The dirt slowly accumulates with each entrant. When man makes sweet-cake on me, my bedding is so thin that I feel this notebook's staples against my back. The only reason that I am fed is to keep my breasts filled and my bottom rounded and desirable. Man thereby feeds me.

I am not deranged, for I know that man spends a hundred rupees to have his bhunnas in my face or in my legs, or two hundred in my brown hole.

I am not deranged. I do not really see gold on my ceiling when I look up and I do not smell perfumes in the air. Neither do I smell the rancid stench of my cell or my bed because I am accustomed to it. I do, however, smell man's smells. No man who visits me is clean; on some I smell their wives' cooking and on others, their perfume. On some men I can taste the lipstick of other kisses that have been placed on his lips hours or minutes before mine.

I am often confused. I am confused as to why day always follows night when there is so much variability in everything else. I am confused about why beauty resides in variability rather than in constancy. I suppose that there must be forces that exceed my ability to understand them. But that is neither delusion nor insanity.

I am not deranged, but there are countless days I wish I were.

17

~

I arrived in Mumbai with Father. During the week before we left, there was an unusual hush at home and so I knew something was up. Mother and Father did not argue even once, and there were no whiffs of perfume on Father's sweat-drenched work clothes. I knew too that somehow I was responsible for this tranquillity, in part because Mother was kind to me even when she should not have been. Father was different; there was a new sad feeling between us that I later came to realize was regret.

I am now an expert on the regret of men. Regret does not obey the rules of class or money. The husband, priest, father, teacher, doctor, businessman, son, banker, thief, politician all have the capacity for regret. From that day Father showed me his capacity for regret, I came to recognize it in all the men I met. When the soy farmers need to protect their crops from the harsh sun, they use veils of white plastic cloth with string woven through it; despite being lightweight and almost transparent, it is indestructible. Entire fields are swathed in this material, which resembles enormous sails. The white fluttering sails do not stop the sun from entering and making the crops grow; the clarity and intensity of the sun is dulled, however. This is true of regret. It is a veil, and like all human emotions it serves to soften the impact of reality. It is a failed belief that we cannot experience the true brilliance of the light, but it is through fear that we veil ourselves from that brilliance.

We cloak ourselves in layers upon layers of regret, dishonesty, cruelty, and pride. Father, the week he brought me to Mumbai, was veiled in regret.

I found out that I was leaving for Mumbai when I attended my goodbye party. It was not like a birthday party but rather was a gathering of people who were all uneasy. No one knew what to do or say and I did not get any presents. Everyone there, except me, knew that I was leaving. As the sweet-cakes and biscuits were passed around and the bowls of dahl slopped out, we were not burned by the afternoon sun, as the entire village was shrouded in a thick veil of regret.

Everyone said goodbye to me. My brothers, sisters, and cousins cried and my baby brother Avijit wept. As I tried to work out what was happening, I decided that I was ill. I thought I was going to die from some disease that no one would tell me about.

When Mother explained to me that Father was going to take me to Mumbai I therefore

19

assumed it was to see a doctor, although normally we would go to Bhopal for serious medical matters. I concluded that I must be terminally ill. Then everything made sense: the party, the tears, Mother's kindness, and Father's gloominess. I became scared, which is unusual for me because I am the silver-eyed leopard.

The journey to Mumbai necessitated a great deal of walking and my first journey on a bus — just Father and me. I started out holding Father's hand, chatting with him about the party and giggling about Uncle V, who fell asleep again while eating. By the time we had reached the main road my hair was sweaty and dusty and my hand separate from Father's. Father and I shared few words as we waited for the bus. We sat in the shade of a dull green woody tree that had spent its entire life waiting for buses.

Father sat looking outward with his back against the tree, his knees bent and his feet flat against the red-brown sand in front of him. He stared out across crops cloaked in white sheeting. The landscape was speckled with occasional trees that stood either alone or in groupings of two or three. The heat was excessive and the sky was a pale blue. After about ten seconds of watching my silent, folded-up father, I started to unwrap the food bundle that Mother had given me. She had wrapped several delicacies in a red-and-green square of cotton that I recognized from our hut. My eyes lit up; there were sweet-breads, nan breads, chutneys, and relishes (they were all leftovers from the party). Best of all, there were flour balls sweetened with dust-sugar, white sweet-cakes with swirls of green inside, and red sweets sprinkled with sparkling sugar crystals. Each item was so carefully wrapped and so easily unwrapped!

'Batuk,' Father snapped, 'if you eat everything now, you will have nothing for the journey.' 'Hmm,' I said, and then started to munch. The white sweet-bread with the green swirls was delicious. 'Father, why are we going to Mumbai . . . am I ill or something?' 'No, Batuk,' Father said in an irritated tone, 'why would you think that? You are not ill.' I was relieved beyond belief. We sat in silence for a few minutes more and then I asked, 'Then why are we going there . . . where will we stay?'

'Batuk, you will find out soon enough.' Father's voice was dry and he was irritated with me. 'Now be quiet and don't eat anything else — I told you. The bus will be here soon.' I was silent after that.

I decided to get up and talk to the tree. I asked the tree, 'What is it like for you to wait

21

all your life for buses and never get on them when they come?' The tree was initially silent but then answered me a little rudely, 'Did you not hear your father? Be quiet and wait for the bus.' There was a pause, and then the tree realized that I was going to take myself away and leave him alone. He cleared his woody throat. 'You know, Batuk, I could tell you what it is like to wait many lives for many buses . . . but, sweet girl, I am thirsty and can barely talk.' I thought for a moment and cried, 'Wait!' I ran to my bundle, grabbed my skin of water, and ran back to the tree's roots and poured my water over them.

'Batuk!' Father screamed at me. 'What the hell are you doing! Stop! Stop!' 'But Father, the tree is so thirsty. His voice is hoarse,' I answered. Father looked up at me from the ground and his face reddened from his neck upward. He was just about to scream at me again but stopped himself. 'Come here, you little devil,' he called, and opened his arms. I ran over and jumped into Father's arms. His work clothes were soft from their million washings and I could smell Mother's cooking on him. In his arms, I melted into him and became him, for that is what I am — his. He was my father, who was taking me, his silver-eyed leopard, all the way to Mumbai. In the middle of nowhere, under the tree, I shut my eyes. I recognized that everyone's regret at my leaving was only because they wished to be where I was now, in the arms of Father waiting for our bus.

The tree was watching me as Father and I sat there together as one. The tree spoke, 'Batuk, why don't you stay here with me? I could teach you all the mysteries of the world. My leaves have heard the laughter, words, and cries of every living thing. My roots have tasted water from across the earth. My bark holds the map to the secrets of all knowledge. My seed was blown here from a tree in the great garden of the Taj and so I know perfect love too. Come, Batuk, leave your father and melt into me.'

'But tree,' I said from my father's arms, 'you know everything there is to know, and still you stay here waiting for a bus but never get on it. So what is your service?' 'My service,' said the tree, 'is to provide you with shade.' I thought about this in the long silence that followed, Father having fallen asleep. I wiggled out of Father's arms and went over to the tree and scrutinized its bark. All I could see were little insects crawling in the crevices and cracks. Some insects seemed to have purpose and others wandered hither and fro, but they were all just insects scurrying around on a great tree. I said to the tree, 'I cannot stay with you. I must go with Father to Mumbai on the bus.'

I saw the distant cloud of dust from our bus approaching. 'Father, Father, our bus!' Father woke up and started to collect his few things as the bus approached. The tree said to me, 'I have one more thing to tell you, Batuk.' There was no malice in the tree's voice, just regret. 'Yes, great tree?' I asked. The tree answered in a voice so soft that you had to concentrate intensely on his leaves to hear it, 'The whole world, Batuk, was created for you alone and no other.'

As I turned to Father I noticed that the water I had poured over the tree's roots had risen to Father's face, for there I saw it, dripping from his eyes.

~

I had never been on a bus before. The bus driver was the fattest man in the world, next to Uncle V. He wore a light blue patterned shirt unbuttoned to his mid-chest. He had breasts bigger than Mother's and appeared to have a spare meal, or at least snacks, sprinkled over them. He was squished into the driver's chair and you could see that the springs were fully compressed to the point

24

where they no longer sprang. The chair had once been coated in red vinyl but was now so patchy and worn that the stuffing exuded from it like pus from a boil. I was amazed that the driver could turn the steering wheel at all, as his belly squashed against it so hard that the white plastic wheel was enfolded in his flesh.

As we started to climb up the steps of the bus, the driver turned his huge head downward and barked, 'What the shit are you two doing? If you are getting on, get on with it. If you are going to stay here and rot, get the hell off my bus.' Each of his cheeks hung off his face and wobbled as he spoke, as if he had two nan breads stapled below his eyelids. 'And what do we have here?' he asked, looking at me as I scurried up behind Father. I noticed that only his left eye moved. He farted and growled, 'Rat-Bag, what do they call you?' He had not shaved his face for days and I was sure I could see gravy on his chin hair.

I said, 'My name is Batuk.' 'Batuk Rat-Bag, what sort of name is that? Where is your tail?' He laughed at his joke. He said to Father, 'You look like a cheapskate — I bet you want to land your asses on the roof . . . if I lose the Rat-Bag on a turn . . . then that's a bloody pity but don't come crying to me.'

Father was counting out his money as the

driver looked me up and down, rather like he was examining a snack. Then he curled his slightly bluish lips and asked, 'So you think you can hang on, Rat-Bag Patook?' I looked at the floor and said, 'I bet you couldn't throw me off if you wanted to. This piece of junk doesn't go fast enough.' (If Mother had been there she would have slapped me.) He squeezed out of his chair, which was an astonishing feat since he was so tightly packed in; I thought the steering wheel might snap off. It crossed my mind that the driver might not have gotten out of his chair in a long time because he was actually a part of the bus, rather like the exhaust pipe. This thought was interrupted as he bellowed, 'What the shit did you say?' He farted on the *Wh*.

As he shouted, the entire air mass of the bus vibrated. He looked out at the array of scattered passengers, most of whom were trying to look elsewhere. 'Ladies and gentlemen who are the esteemed and most honored passengers of the I.B.C., today you are in for a damn treat. Rat-Bag Patook does not believe that I can shake her from my bus . . . All I can say is that she should be ready for a long walk to Mumbai. When I get a rat on my bus I make sure to shake it off.' As he laughed I was sure I could smell his curry from long past. Several of the peasant passengers hooted and applauded. But then my father spoke, a short, slight man standing before the giant ball of ghee. He spoke in a barely audible voice at a painfully slow speed. 'Dear sir,' he began, and you could sense the tree listening through the open windows. As each word left Father's lips, I became more incredulous. Father said, 'It is quite possible that you will drive this bus so recklessly as to place a nine-year-old girl in peril of her life. But the next time you call my daughter Rat-Bag, I will remove the tongue from your mouth and put it in your lunch box.'

If someone had told me what would happen next, I would never have believed it. In an instantaneous action, Father pulled his khukri knife from behind his back, where I did not even know he had it. It was the curved knife he uses in the fields to cut plants, crack the ground, and decapitate snakes. What amazed me even more than the knife itself was the rock-like steadiness with which Father held the nine-inch blade against the driver's sagging neck and his apparent intent to use it. His hand did not waver even a grass-breadth and his eyes showed no emotion except a bored calm. The bus driver had stopped breathing and there was absolute silence on the bus; even the tree had stopped moving.

'We should leave for Mumbai,' Father whispered to the driver, and as he lowered the blade the driver's head bobbled up and down in agreement. Father bought two third-class tickets, which are the best tickets there are. You get to sit on top of the bus and see everything. As we drove off I waved goodbye to the tree.

The long ride to Mumbai was magical. Together Father and I watched Madhya Pradesh disappear. We pointed things out to each other: a vulture, a dead horse, thin cows, and funny-looking people. We drank sherbets at rest stops, dozed occasionally, and ate all our supplies. Father laughed many times. I thought that I did not really know him as a man but only as a father. He was a man of impulse and passion; so much of him was hidden from me. Father's uncontrollable, unassailable, indivisible, unquantifiable love for me had emerged in a momentary act of violence. 'Thank you,' I said, as Father offered me a piece of mango he had cut with his khukri knife.

~

Father feared that reports of the driver being threatened at knifepoint would arrive in

28

Mumbai before us. When the bus stopped in traffic at the outer limits of the city, we scrambled down the ladder to the street.

We entered an area that was a sea of makeshift huts. The huts looked similar to those back home and I suspect that many of the people who live there came from villages like ours. There were rivers and rivulets of these dwellings. Why would people leave the fields to come here? The dogs, cats, and rats looked mangy, scavenging around us much like their two-legged masters. The air was warm and moist and smelled of rotting garbage and human excrement. A harmony of shrieking metal-wheeled carts, barking dogs, and the buzz of decay was accompanied by a gentle rhythm of human noise.

With nowhere to sleep, Father found a small unused space between two family huts and unrolled the maroon blanket he carried. Both families watched him in silence and no one objected to our vagrancy. Father told me to stay still until he returned with food. I had been sitting on the bus for most of the day, and I was exhausted. I lay on our blanket staring at the zigzagging white patterns that pierced the woven maroon sky. I was thinking of nothing. My nose had already adapted to the stench, and the sky was darkening.

Suddenly, in front of me appeared two thin

ankles and I looked up. A boy about my age was staring down at me with the same expression as if he had spotted a strange piece of scrap metal on the floor. I felt he was wondering what potential use I had. His clothes were rags whereas mine were simple — a little sand-soiled but otherwise clean. He cocked his head to the right, wrinkled his brow, inhaled, and was about to speak, but the words he was thinking never came. He then spontaneously turned away from me and sprinted off into the morass of huts without looking back. I sat up to watch him disappear. It occurred to me that his actions were the same as those of the dogs who follow their swaying noses into a garbage pile, realize that there is nothing left to eat, and run elsewhere seeking food. This is the behavior of the hungry but not of the starving. The starving stop, lie down, and prepare to die. The hungry scavenge.

~

There he is, Prince Puneet. Puneet walks from his nest into the Common Street for the first time in days. When waiting to bake, we are permitted to hop between nests under the yellow gaze of the sunning Hippopotamus.

30

Puneet is unsure of his legs. He is not wearing any makeup and when he sees me, his face explodes in a smile. 'Batuk, Batuk!' he cries, and runs to me despite the obvious discomfort that I can see in his eyes. I throw down my book and my ever-shortening pencil (I will need a solution for that) and rush toward him. I hold him tight and, oh, he does have a faint odor of manhood. We speak at the same time, laugh, and try again. I whisper in his ear, 'Heh, careful, do not look too well, my prince, otherwise you will have to make sweet-cake today.' Puneet is happy to hold me and rocks me in his embrace. 'Hippo told me I am working tonight anyway. So what do I care?' he asks. 'I have been feeling great for a few days anyway.' His smile is stretched across his beautifully defined face, from which his boy cheeks are disappearing. I am still holding him as I answer, 'I have so missed you.' I place a thin smile on my face and gaze upward into his eyes. 'Not as much as my man-fuckers,' he responds. 'Puneet!' I cry, pretending to be shocked, 'how can you speak that way, my holy, holy prince . . . are you . . . are you . . . ' I am not sure quite how to ask but he understands. He holds me at arm's length and says, laughing at me, 'Oh, I know what you mean. Can I still shake my ass and bring in the rupees?' He grins. 'The

31

doctor says I am all right . . . you should have seen the smile on Mamaki's face.'

We stop talking, he lets me go, and we take each other's hands to form our own little circle, and look at each other. He flicks his head as if to restart his motor and asks, 'What is that you are doing with that book and pencil . . . are you keeping records on me?' 'No,' I say with a hint of artifice flooding my cheeks, 'I am writing.' 'I did not know you could write, you sly little fox. What are you writing?' he asks. 'I am writing about how I came to Mumbai and fell head over heels in love with you, oh Prince Puneet of my dreams.'

Puneet half skips in the air as he laughs out loud in a bright, singing laugh and answers, 'Batuk, you are my brain, my heart, my hands. You know that you are my only love. That little notebook can never contain even an ounce of my love for you.' I parry, 'Soon, my beloved, you will be able to love me as a king, rather than as a prince,' and with that I drop my eyes down his chest to his groin. He is not flushed for a second and answers with a loud laugh. 'This,' he says, pointing to his bhunnas, 'is only for you, my beloved.'

Puneet snatches my book and runs (wincing) to the entrance to his nest, where he sits down. He opens my notebook and

32

turns the pages one by one, knitting his brow and nodding his head. He looks up at me. 'I am marvelous and beautiful, you say.' 'Oh, that's not all,' I respond. 'Turn over and see on the next page . . . can you see? I write that you composed Shiva's songs and that he fell in love with you.' He turns the page, stares at it, and nods. I laugh. 'I know you can't read, you stupid pretty boy.' He slaps the book shut, frowns, jumps up, and tries to smack my bottom with the book. 'Stupid — you call me . . . you will pay for that!' He grabs me and my eyes dance with his.

This is how we talk: two prostitutes on the Common Street in Mumbai.

～

I was falling asleep on the maroon blanket when Father returned with a bowl of rice, dripping, and bread. 'What a wonderful city,' he cried out with a huge smile on his face, 'all of this and a beer for five rupees.' He was not carrying beer. After we shared the food, Father and I lay on the blanket. He held me curled into him, his tummy to my back. I slept well, adrift on a sea of scavengers.

I woke up amid the gentle crashing waves

of a world starting to dart frenetically around me. As I wiped the crinkles from my eyes, I could see that Father was anxious to leave. We had a business appointment to attend and it was clear that being late was not an option; 'Important business,' Father had said. As Father ventured out into the city streets I noticed that he seemed overwhelmed. I, on the other hand, was mesmerized. I had never seen cars sitting in line with people inside them. How they loved to sound their hooters. Why were children in uniform; were they in prison? Each time we got lost, there was more to see. For a while, I became fascinated by the patterns the paving stones made; I would see shapes hidden there and try to decode their secrets. Color was everywhere — in people's clothes as they crammed on tiny buses, in the fields of washing hung to dry in the open-air laundry, in the stores, and even in the heaps of rubbish. The city's air was not only infused with smells, fumes, and dust but also a soup of color.

Father kept a blistering pace as we walked across the city, mostly lost. Oftentimes it was not his speed or irritability that bothered me but rather my need to stop frequently and examine all that pulsated around me. On one occasion, I was riveted to the spot watching a train packed with passengers speed through the city on rails suspended high in the air. It was as though the train flew through the sky. I was desperately hoping to see someone fall off but no one did. Father broke this moment of suspended time with a wrenching pull on my arm and off we set to become lost — yet again.

After getting lost almost a dozen times and Father becoming ever more frustrated, we arrived at our destination. I had forgotten to be tired and climbed up the light brown brick steps behind Father. The steps were each so high that I had to almost jump up onto the next. Father was clutching an address written on a small, crumpled piece of paper like a bird holds on to a captured grasshopper.

At the top of the stairwell was a tall dark brown door with a metal ring handle as large as my head, held in the mouth of a dark metal lion. Father pounded the ring onto the door. It clearly required all the strength of the young woman opening the door to move it. Once we had entered, I turned back to see her throwing her shoulder onto the door to close it. We stood in a long, dark hallway, which was lit by a single glass chandelier hanging from the ceiling. The stone floor was covered by a faded yellow-and-red carpet. On the left side of the hallway, against the wall, were two chairs, and between them stood a long, narrow table. On the table was a wooden box inlayed with what appeared to be gold.

The other end of the hallway was shielded by a hanging curtain. We stood waiting in the hallway, a closed door behind us, and the curtain ahead of us hiding the path forward.

A booming voice called from far beyond the curtain deep inside the building. 'You are late, Mr. Ramasdeen. We were expecting you before lunch.' My father shouted an apology to a man who was not yet visible but who was obviously moving toward us with haste. I could hear his puffing and his pounding steps as he moved closer.

Master Gahil, as I would learn was his name, burst through the hanging red curtain at the end of the hallway. The curtain had small silvered mirrors and bells sewn into it and so his entrance was echoed by a montage of darting light and tinkling. 'There she is,' he called out. Looking down at me, his large face erupted with pleasure. I felt he was about to eat me.

Master Gahil turned his head and screamed toward the curtain, 'Kumud, come immediately. My baby niece from the fields has arrived and she is filthy.' My hitherto unknown uncle was portly and exuded the sheen of self-importance. He was wearing clothes I had only heard about in stories, several layers of garments, all of which were trimmed in gold. His undercoat was white; another layer was red velvet. He wore a handwoven short vest jacket and a light-weight white topcoat with intricate patterns sewn in gold thread. Overall, he was a carefully crafted ball of glittering color and billowing material.

An old, stooped woman shuffled into the room, her feet sliding against the carpet with a *whoosh — whoosh — whoosh*. Her head was cast downward and even when she turned toward Master Gahil, she moved with the glue of aging. Her plain blue sari was worn as a simple garment by a woman who understood the simplicity of her position in the world.

The woman's expression was that of an imploring old dog asking her master for scraps of meat. Master Gahil spoke to her as if she were a dog. 'Kumud, take little Batuk here and clean her up. Also, tell Dr. Dasdaheer to be here tomorrow morning.' He looked me up and down and again smiled. He shouted, 'Go now!' and bade the old woman away with a wave of his arm. She slowly turned and began to walk in her stooped way toward the curtain. In a smooth practiced action that caught me unawares, she grasped me by the scruff of my tunic and dragged me with her. For an old woman, her strength was astounding. Father called out, 'Batuk, it's my fault; I lost everything . . . darling, wait,' and moved toward me. Master Gahil bellowed, 'You should have thought of this silliness, Mr. Ramasdeen, when you decided to be so late. We have business to complete and I have to go out this evening.' Turning to the shuffling servant woman, he shouted, 'Old woman, take her immediately. I do not have time for this nonsense.'

As Master Gahil thrust a pregnant envelope into Father's tensed hand, I saw a familiar expression dart across Father's face. I recognized it instantly from our trips to the doctor he invented to hide his lavender-perfumed 'cousin' from Mother: self-loathing veiled in lust. As I observed the depth of my father's weakness, our gazes touched and from him I felt the kiss of inner death. I was transfixed as I felt him draw me within him in terror.

But our circle snapped. In shock seasoned with panic, I was propelled by the surprising force of the old woman and was thrust through to the other side of the silver curtain. The last words I would ever hear from my father were, 'Batuk . . . darling . . . my silver-eyed leopard.' The last words Father ever heard from me were, 'Daddy, take your Batuk — I beg of you.'

~

With Puneet unwell, I had anticipated that I would receive more of Mamaki's attention than usual. My prediction was right, but I had failed to fully calculate its impact. 'My darling, I have more time to love you now' was her way of expressing this state of affairs. I had overheard several of Mamaki's conversations with Master Gahil and I realized that Mamaki was expected to generate the same income from the six of us, regardless of Puneet's indisposition. One afternoon I heard Gahil say to Hippopotamus, 'I know, dearest Mother Briila, how difficult it is with the boy out of commission, and I appreciate very greatly how you dedicate your life to your little ones. But you have to understand that I run a business and I have many responsibilities and obligations. Even I have had to cut back on my essentials with the boy out of action . . . and so, dear Mother Briila, you may have to also.' Within ten minutes of Master Gahil's departure, Mamaki was on the street cajoling men with promises of unheralded pleasures. She doubled her money gifts to the taxi drivers to bring us business, often sweetened with a free excursion or two on our beds. We have been busy. Thank goodness Puneet is returning to work.

Initially, making sweet-cake was not something I tried to excel at. I viewed my baking as a means of survival. Man came upon my throne; I defrocked him and *boom*, all was done. Next please. However, as I matured I realized the fault in this approach.

Look at it this way. Say your mother makes you clean the clothes for yourself and your brothers and sisters. You want to get the job done as quickly as possible so that you can go and play. So you grab the clothes in your arms and run down to the river with a soap bar. You throw them in the water and clean them as quickly as possible. You wring out the clothes, throw them over the hot afternoon rocks to dry, and an hour or two later, you gather them up in a bundle and bring them back to the house. You then throw them in a bundle on the floor in the middle of the room. The clothes have been cleaned! Job done! But then how Mother scolds you. 'You are not playing tonight, they are still filthy,' she screams. The slap on your face lingers long after the hunger fades from another missed supper.

Now look at it differently. The objective is the same. 'Batuk, go wash the clothes.' But this time I decide to do this with excellence. (Why? you may ask. Wait and see). Off I go. I walk down to the riverbank and sort first through the clothes. I identify those with particularly nasty stains and put them in one pile, and identify those that are particularly fine and put them in another pile. I then wash all the clothes and make an extra effort with the stained ones; I am more careful with the delicate ones so that they do not tear. After an extra rinse and wringing the clothes out, I lay them on the rocks and nap for a couple of hours. I then carefully fold all the clothes, organize the trousers in one pile, shirts in another, and bring them up to the house. 'Mother,' I say, 'look! I really tried to get that dirt stain out of this blouse . . . ' Mother looks at the neat pile and cannot help but smile, squeeze my cheek (in love), and kiss my head. Furthermore, I notice an extra dollop of dahl at supper-time and harmony in the air. She says, 'Darling, why don't you go and play tomorrow. Your sister can wash clothes.'

Now you understand. In both cases I completed the task. In the first case, I had to wash the clothes twice. I was slapped and went to bed hungry. In the second case, I washed the clothes so slowly that I napped on the rocks all afternoon and went to bed with a full tummy and a kiss. I got to play all the next evening. I hate cleaning clothes (hate it) but in the second case it was less hateful than it might have been.

So too with man. On one hand, you can view my objective as being purely functional, the sole charge being to make sweet-cake without any care for its appearance or taste. Here you are! Sweet-cake — one hundred rupees.

On the other hand, say you carefully prepare the ingredients, make them enticing, colorful, and varied, and then let the student only taste the sugar one crystal at a time until he is salivating and desperate with hunger. Say you then show him how to knead the dough, and guide him to slowly roll in a little egg white, sugar, and color. He then is taught that the longer the kneading, the tastier the sweet-cake. Soon, he is relaxed and kneading away, buying more and more different types of ingredients and taking longer and longer doing it. There is a harmonious feeling from the cooking, which smells good. With all this time in preparation, he is happy to patiently watch the dough rise and wait out a longer baking time. Sometimes the baking process itself becomes so beguiling that man does not even wait until the sweet-cake leaves the oven, as he is satisfied enough. For those who wait it out, when the sweet-cake comes from the oven, how happy they are and how grateful. The sweet-cake melts in their mouth and swamps their emotions with its warmth. They leave with smiles. Later, they return for more enchanting sweet-cake and they are prepared to pay greatly for it so that they may cook the finest sweet-cake of their lives. By enhancing the sweet-cake experience as I do, I make Mamaki so happy with me that she smiles and kisses me, gives me finer clothes, fresher makeup, and richer food. Most important of all, I end up having to make less sweet-cake overall — for I hate making sweet-cake for man, hate it.

In fact, that is how I came to write today's note in ink. One of my favorite students comes on the same day each week, as regular as clockwork. Like many of my students, he regards me as if I were a favorite niece or even one of his daughters. Knowing Mamaki's current predicament regarding our income, we cook the longest, most delicious (most expensive) sweet-cake you can imagine. Afterward, I brush his hair, the little that there is, and he slides on his jacket, ready to leave.

I see it in his pocket, the blue pen. I gasp.

43

He inquires, 'What is it?' I explain. He is shocked. 'A simple Biro, really? You want it?' 'Yes . . . yes, please.' 'Of course, take it.' A kiss. He leaves. Hide pen in mattress. It is mine. Mamaki pours in. A pause. A gigantic smile. 'Batuk — darling — you are the greatest of my loves — I do so love you.' A kiss. A sniff of her rancid body. My pen — safe.

~

I can hardly claim that I am exhausted as a result of Puneet's indisposition. However, of course, I have been pretending that I am. Puneet is back at work and we are all reaping the benefits. What is more, he seems happy again, having reaffirmed his position as number one. As the only boy of the six of us and, in fact, the only long-term boy on the street, Puneet is worth two or three of us. Bakers will sometimes stand in line to wait for him; he is a magnet. He is also stupid.

Puneet has less history than I do. He came from the fields with his whole family when he was tiny; he was the youngest of the children (I am the second oldest in our family but the eldest of the girls). He told me that he was always beautiful, even as a baby, which I can

44

well believe. He lost his family when his father was caught stealing from a building site. His father had pilfered some lumber (forty-seven planks by hand!) and resold it to another builder, and when he was caught he was sent to prison. Puneet's mother only had her looks to support her three children with; she did not have enough money for the bus fare back to her village and so became a friend to lonely men to feed her family. One night she went out with a wealthy regular friend of hers and never returned. Puneet remembers that her friend wore a white suit and had a shining silver belt buckle and gave the children sweets whenever he came. Thereafter, Puneet was an orphan.

Perhaps it is because his parents were stupid that Puneet is so stupid. For at least a year Puneet has begged or even stolen extra favors from his clients. He told me that sometimes he just asks them, 'A little something extra, master.' On other occasions, he will take the wallet from a sleeping baker, lift a hundred rupees, and then return the wallet. Of course he always tells me; he says that when he has saved a thousand rupees he will run away to England or America. I laugh. 'Probably in an airplane you buy in the Street of Thieves,' I tease him. 'Ooooh, princess,' he will say, 'boys with my talent make a lot of money in America. You just watch me.' He has told me this dream so many times, I know it better than he does.

Pah! The ending is always the same: Mamaki finds his hidden stash every time. Mind you, where are you going to hide bundles of money in a cell the size of a single ox? Where in your body can you hide a coil of bank notes? Does he not realize that it only takes one client to tell Mamaki and she will raid him? He is so predictable that I bet she just waits a few weeks and raids him anyway. Either way, he is always left with nothing.

What I find difficult to understand is that Puneet stays — for he does not have to. He is a fourteen-year-old boy with muscle and a beautiful way about him. He can outrun Hippopotamus, the other matrons, and Ranjit, the sadist guard. Once loose, he will never be spotted among the thousands of boys in the city. Were he to leave Mumbai, he would disappear.

In general, the only time Puneet is sad is after he has been raided and has had his cash stripped from him. That is when I say to him, 'Why don't you run — you could do it.' He always answers the same. 'But, princess, how can I breathe a breath without you beside me?' He is stupid and a coward. Just as he is afraid to face freedom, he is also afraid to end the cycle he and Mamaki are caught up in. He knows that she will find his hidden money, just as she knows he will hide it. He knows that she needs him and I guess at least that is something.

After the policemen ripped his brown hole, I thought that once he recovered, Puneet would finally be ready to run. The opposite transpired, perhaps because they ripped his mind apart too. He seems happier now than he ever has been. He is puffed up, bedecked in his scarlet, gold-trimmed sari, his pale blue eye makeup, and his cherry-red lips. I watch him draped against the entranceway of his nest welcoming a novice as if he were an old friend. I hold my breath waiting for him to lash out, but somehow he does not. Puneet's beautiful boy body has melted into his nest. Like a piece of used furniture, he belongs there, but he forgets that used furniture can be cast out in a second to be replaced with the new.

That was last night. The world can change in a day, or even a second.

~

While Puneet was recovering from the policemen's assault, Master Gahil and Mamaki had

47

engaged in a series of quiet conversations, most of which I overheard, as neither of them has the capacity to speak softly. Although most of the talk related to the lost earnings due to Puneet's illness, one late night, after business, when Gahil came for the night's takings, he spoke for a long time with Mamaki about Puneet. It was clear to Master Gahil that Puneet's advancing puberty could prove problematic, although Mamaki was less concerned.

The outcome of these meetings became clear last night. Just before dawn, I was awakened by headlamps shining into my nest. Puneet yelped as he was thrown into a dark blue van. It happened in seconds. I understand that his castration also only took seconds.

Puneet returned five days later, an empty vessel. Destruction hung over him like Father's khukri knife poised over the swirling head of a snake trapped under his foot; the end was upon him. He had bandages wrapped across his groin. I knew, now, that he would never run away.

~

Puneet always used to laugh at me when I called what a man did 'making sweet-cake.'

He would throw open his mouth and laugh out loud. He would taunt me, 'So what's in the oven, princess?'

The expression was born two days after Father left me at Master Gahil's house. The moment I arrived there was the moment I left Father's. The old woman, Kumud, put me in what she called 'my room' and started to close the door. She leaned into the room and spoke so quietly that I had to stop weeping to hear her. 'When you have control, I will feed you.' I knew that this moment was a break point between my past and my future; my screams and sobs were rather like a full stop ending one sentence at the same time it starts another. I had begun to adapt to my abandonment the moment I left the village, and by the time I reached this room, I was in some way prepared to be left there. Even now, I recognize that the young adapt fast. Inexperience or purity is a blessing, since a virgin-white picture has never had shapes, shade, or color painted on it. It is far easier to paint on a blank canvas than on one that has already been painted on.

I became transformed as I lay on that bed, which was the most luxurious I had ever felt. When clay dries in an oven, it is changed from a soft, malleable form to a solid, defined one; once baked, the hardened clay can never be molded again, only broken. A few hours earlier I had entered Gahil's house as a soft glob of warm clay. I would leave there a hardened, useful vessel.

After I had channeled enough energy into crying and screaming, I was hungry and so I stopped crying. In my silence, I looked around me; the bed was large enough for all my brothers and sisters to sleep on, and it was so high off the ground that to reach the floor, I had to jump. Covering it was a blanket sewn with flowers. It remained light outside but two electric lamps were switched on, both of which had ornate, pale pink lampshades, so the room's light had a tinge of gentility. Bolted to the ceiling was a slow-turning fan with five large white sails, and I could feel the soft breeze on my cheeks. If you stared at it for long enough, the fan could hypnotize you. There were several pieces of wooden furniture in the room: two chairs, a chest of drawers, and two bedside tables. All the furniture was so well polished that it shone and reflected the light beams. The window was open and I could hear the sounds of the street outside: the cars, the cries, and the barks. It was the first time I had ever seen bars across a window.

I heard the lock in the door click, and the door gradually opened. In shuffled the old woman. Were it not for the fact that she moved forward with excruciating slowness (*pshhh, pshhh, pshhh*), I would have taken her for dead. She did not blink, she did not say anything, and her face was stiff like the leather of a worn saddle. When she did eventually speak, I could have sworn that her lips did not move and her voice sounded like the speaking dead. Dead or not, she carried a tray of food.

She placed the tray on top of the chest of drawers. I pretended to be uninterested but could not stop myself from peering at it. There was fruit, a tan curry, a bowl of dahl, and sweet-cakes like you have never seen. The sweet-cakes were green, blue, and red, oval, flat, and cone-shaped. I inhaled the entire plate of sweet-cakes and with a little less self-control I would have eaten the plate as well. I did not touch the curry or dahl until all the sweet-cakes were gone, and then I ate those too. While I fulfilled my hunger, the old woman disappeared (or had I eaten her?).

Pshhh, pshhh, pshhh — she returned a few minutes later with a white towel. 'Come with me,' she croaked. Then I did, in retrospect, what any nine-year-old would do: I threw a bolt of defiance. I sat down on the floor, *plump*, brought my knees to my chin, and gave the old woman a look of absolute resolve. 'No,' I said, 'I will not move until you bring me more sweet-cakes.' She did not engage my gaze, or appear to have heard my demand. Her only response was to kick me.

Part of getting old is that you become scrawny, which must be why when they kill a goat at the last moment before its natural death, it tastes like wood. The old woman did not have a single ounce of flesh on her leg. It felt as though I were being kicked by a human table leg. What is more, Table Leg kicked with venom and it hurt like hell.

She bade me follow her for a second time, and this time I obeyed. We shuffled along the corridor and entered a room, in the middle of which was a large white container filled with steaming hot water. When she told me to get into it, I assumed she was going to cook me. I had never been immersed in hot water before, having always cleaned myself in the river. The heat was scalding but it was a different heat from lying on the rocks by the river. My fears were heightened when she started to pour fragrant oil into the water — I immediately started looking for the rice. She pushed her sari off her arms and grasped, in her thin, talonlike hands, the hugest tablet of soap I have ever seen. She leaned over the steaming tub of water and started to clean me.

Of course I had been cleaned by my mother or an aunt, but never like this. The old woman had remarkable strength in her bony hands. With the soap and a scratchy yellow cloth, she scraped a layer of skin off every part of my body. Each time I screamed, she scrubbed harder, until I realized the folly of crying out. I think she was quite disappointed not to find any lice in my hair, because she inspected my head twice. When she was satisfied she told me to climb out of the tub. I stood naked before her, expecting her to offer me the towel she held in her hands. She did not do so immediately, though, but allowed me to drip on the floor. Under her folded eyelids I saw her gaze move. Her eyes were small and dark blue; the whites of her eyes had yellowed like milk aged into cheese. She looked me over from hair to hand, from breast to knee, and from groin to foot. Her eyes covered every inch of me. At that moment, with no understanding of what was to befall me, I felt connected with this decrepit sadist. We were equally trapped in our roles; I as a victim and she as the oppressor. Neither of us had chosen our paths and in another life our current roles might be reversed. Nonetheless, we had both gravitated to this moment together.

I walked back into the room draped in a

towel. The door behind me locked. I went to bed naked, my hair only half dry. I was clean.

~

Last night I had my dream again. I rarely dream but when I do, the dream is often the same one. It is about a hat vendor. I can never work out why some nights I dream and some nights I do not. I always eat the same food, work the same work, live in the same space, but sometimes I dream.

In my dream I am walking through a roofed market, along a corridor of pale yellow stone that extends downward as far as I can see. On both sides of the corridor are stalls that sell everything you would expect: vegetables, dresses, toys, spices, and devotional carvings. However, there are other stalls that sell strange items, such as pieces of people's bodies desiccated by the sun, the carcass of our old cow somehow miniaturized and preserved (nothing else is sold in that stall), severed but moving hands and feet, and clothes that speak. The market is crowded with people of all different sizes pushing against one another. Along the entire length of the rooftop, descending down into the market, is my hair.

I enter the market from the top and walk down the middle of the path. As I walk, my hair falls from the ceiling and curls on my head like a growing, shining black turban. The people divide as I walk through the market and everybody touches me as I pass them. Some hold out their hands to brush against me; others strain just to touch me with their fingertips. Still others grope my breasts, my belly, and my legs. No one touches my face, and I feel that as I breathe out, they inhale as one giant being. My breath becomes the finest mist of rain, and by inhaling it they fill themselves with me.

As I walk down through the market, at first I feel brilliant. As I walk further, though, I feel increasingly weakened and thirsty. My throat sometimes feels so parched that I have to resist waking up. Then, on my right, I see a hat stall. The hat stall sells only the straw hats of the field that the men wear all day long to farm. They are neatly stacked in many piles to form a wall from the floor to the ceiling. The hat vendor is behind the wall of hats and cannot be seen. Although I am thirsty, I cry out, almost as if I am singing, 'Honored sir, can I please buy a hat from you?' He replies from behind the wall, 'But they are not for ladies of your station.' I beg, 'Please, please, my lord, sell me a hat.'

Suddenly, the wall of hats is pushed out at me and the piles of hats flood over me. 'Help!' I cry. The hats are falling everywhere. They are tumbling down the market street. The other people keep walking downward through the market and stomp over them. I cry out in panic and scurry on the floor, desperately trying to pick up all the hats. The hat vendor starts to laugh, a deep-pitched, joyous laugh. He calls out to me, 'Run, Batuk, gather them up. Oh look, another one has fallen — grab it.' My arms are constantly full of hats, but as I reach down to pick one up, two spill out of my arms back onto the floor. I bend over to pick up the fallen hats, but then more fall still. I fear the wrath of the hat vendor. But he is laughing; what is more, his laughter is taking on a musicality and is gaining a rhythm. Finally, I have all the hats balanced in my arms and I turn carefully so as not to let them fall. Just as I come face-to-face with the vendor, I awaken.

~

This morning I woke up with the early light pushing through my nest's curtain. It is cloudy overhead and the light is a diffused orange and the air is cool. I lie on my throne listening to the tumbling of the barrows going to the market and to the rumbling of cars and trains starting the day's traffic. I think of the brother and five sisters with whom I share my life here. I think of how unfair I have been to Meera, for she is so new to the family and very young. I think a lot about Puneet and know that he is forever of the street and that hope has been cut from his body. My mind drifts to my fantasy that one day a cook will want me to bake sweet-cake with him alone and forever. I pray to whoever listens that he will bring a leash to my neck and that I will be led from here to serve him. I pray that he will let me take my pen and my book with me. I am not sure why I write but in my mind I shudder that it may be so that one day I can look back and read how I have melted into my ink and become nothing — become his. You can never fully straighten bent metal; you can only make it less bent.

~

All of us on the Common Street remember our induction, which gave us the right to call ourselves 'a taken one.' When I woke up the first morning after I was left with Master Gahil, I was disoriented, but only for a couple of seconds. I immediately remembered where I was. The old woman had scrubbed my skin so hard that I felt raw lying naked on the soft sheet. I can still remember the softness of those sheets.

I could also hear the activity of the street below. I jumped out of bed and ran across the room naked. I dragged a chair over to the window, stood on it, and stared out. It was early in the day; the gray of the night was being burned away by the morning sun. Cars and trucks drove past, people were milling on the streets, and store owners were preparing their shops for the day. The bakery was already open. My hands held the cool iron bars of the open window; I did not think to cry out. I looked for Father and he was not there.

Hours passed and I started playing 'bouncy-bouncy' on the bed. It was the springiest bed I had ever come across and I leaped up and down repeatedly. Sometimes I would leap up high, touch the ceiling, and flop down on my belly and then spin onto my back. It seemed forever before the old woman unlocked the door and came in with a man who carried a small, light brown case shaped like a thumb.

'Dr. Dasdaheer is here to visit you,' said the woman without a morning greeting. The doctor was a thin graying man who was not as old as the old woman. He wore a crumpled shirt, brown trousers, and a fraying black leather belt. His shoes were filthy with dust. He spoke quietly. He was someone who said whatever he needed to say to get his bill paid. 'Hello, little girl,' he said, 'I am Dr. Dasdaheer and I am here to check you because your uncle wants you to be well.' I was standing naked on the bed, flushed from the jumping. The doctor sat me on the bed. He asked all sorts of questions I had no idea how to answer. He did not seem concerned or angry with my lack of knowledge as to whether I had survived this illness or experienced that ailment. I told him that my birthday had been three weeks earlier. He proceeded to touch me carefully, prod me here and there, and listen to my chest briefly through his ear tubes. I think he was a little disappointed with how well I was.

I was fed more sweet-cakes — two plates full — and warm milk with honey. I was led back to the bathtub, where the old woman left me to soak in more hot water, but this time she did not scrub me.

That afternoon the old woman brought me crayons and paper. I was drawing a house and a cat when I said to her, 'Can I please go home now?' She was sitting asleep in one of the wooden chairs and half opened her heavy eyes, looked at me, and said, 'No. That will not be possible.' I drew for a while longer and then asked, 'Can I see my father?' She said, 'No.' Just like that. I wanted to ask when he would come to visit, but I did not. Lunch was dahl and sweet-cakes but now I was losing the taste for sweet-cakes and time was starting to hang. The old woman fell back asleep.

An eternity later the old woman woke up and left. After a short while she returned carrying a pile of folded clothes. I had been naked all day. When I wanted to pee, the old woman told me to squat over a white porcelain bowl, which she then carried out and brought back empty. I imagined her tripping and spilling the pee all over herself. I had not needed to do brown but assumed that the process would be the same if I did.

The old woman then dressed me. I put on small undergarments that were so white they must have been painted because I never got anything nearly as white when I used to wash clothes in the river. She sat me down in front of a wooden table with a mirror on it and seated herself next to me. She first applied makeup to my eyes and red to my lips. She rubbed dye on my cheeks and painted henna on my palms like a bride. Her frail, bony hands were incredible to watch; they never wavered or trembled. When she painted a swirl, it was perfect the first time. Her fingers moved with beautiful efficiency. The feeling of the wet paintbrush on my skin was exquisite. When she was done, I stared in the mirror and barely recognized myself under the façade. My cheekbones were as defined as mountain ridges, my eyes shone from black frames, and my lips were full. I gasped at my own vision. I was as beautiful as a human could be.

Brushing out and oiling my hair, the old woman looked at me with a proud emptiness, as if she were finishing the decoration of an ornate piece of pottery. When my eyes caught hers she did not look away; instead her eyes invited me to probe deep within her. Deep, deep inside her all I could see was rubble.

After she finished my hair, for the first time in my life, I was wrapped in a sari. It was orange and red with white and silver threads sewn into it, was as light as a feather, and smelled the same as the oil in the bathwater the night before. I was complete; I felt wrapped like a precious gift. The old woman left me and locked the door behind her. I stared at myself in the mirror. It took a moment to realize that it was me. I tilted my head, raised my wrist, and fanned my fingers; I placed a subtle smile on my face. The image before me changed. I spoke out loud and heard a voice I was familiar with emanating from a face that was foreign. I started to perform animal faces in front of the mirror; the lipstick gave them added comedy. I was halfway through my repertoire when the old goat returned. She only half opened the door, leaned through it, and said, 'Come.' Her tone was different from her previous orders. It was as if she were offering me an invitation rather than commanding me. I got up, said goodbye to the frog in the mirror, and left the room with her.

~

The old woman led me through several corridors before arriving at a large pair of dark wooden doors. She did not knock but turned the door handle and pushed the right-side door open. She indicated with her hooded eyes and a nod of her head that I should walk in.

The first thing I noticed when I entered the room was its smell. It stank of incense and made me feel sick. The room was enormous and dark. In its center sat five men spaced around a rectangular table covered in a white cloth. The table was loaded with silver trays of food, glasses, silver cutlery, and white plates with painted gold rims. Smoke was rising from the table like steam off the river. The men were engaged in loud conversation but as soon as they noticed me they instantly hushed. I only recognized one, Master Gahil, who sat puffing on a cigarette. He spoke loudly from across the room, 'May the heavens be praised, you are truly a divine princess ... my sweet.' He smiled at me, beckoning with his jewelry-weighted arm. 'Come in, come in. Divine princess, why don't you show us a little dance?'

I was stunned. I had not prepared anything and did not know any dances. A couple of the men shuffled their chairs around so that they all were facing me. My heart was racing and bumping against my chest. Since no one spoke and they were all watching me, I started to hop from foot to foot, jingling as I did so. The old woman shuffled toward the back of the room. After I stopped my little performance, the men broke out in hysterics and clapped vigorously. I smiled shyly. One of the men said, 'Gahil, at least you did not claim she was a dancer; I hope you are not going to make her sing ... ' I think the fright coupled with the affront got the better of me — after all, I am a performer — and I

63

said in the voice of a cricket, 'I can sing, sir.' The man who had just spoken looked at me. 'You sweet little thing,' he said, 'go on then, sing us a song.' After a short pause, I started to sing in a voice that was so quiet it was almost smothered by the street noise from the open window. I sang the little bedtime song my grandmother used to sing to us:

Mother river, carry me to the spring of your eternity
My little tail tires but I know the sea bids

I see the worm wiggle on the hook but I must not be tempted
Your wind blows against me but I know I must swim harder

My little body fails, my tail flips and flops
And all I want is to see the ocean before I die.

When I finished, the men applauded enthusiastically with colossal smiles on their faces. I clearly was a success. Master Gahil bellowed, 'Little princess, that was wonderful. Little puppy, come here and give each of your uncles a hug. They love you.'

I smiled a little girl's smile and went to hug my newfound uncles. The first uncle was the one who had requested that I sing. He got up from his chair and I saw he was extremely tall. He bent down and opened his arms, then closed them tightly around me like a fish's mouth snapping shut. He smelled of cigarettes. My face was squished against his tummy. He rubbed my back, then kissed my head and muttered something I could not hear while he stroked my hair.

'Come here,' said the second uncle. This uncle was fat and smelled dirty. He did not get up from his chair but pulled me to him and hugged me briefly. He then loosened his grip, took one hand off my back, and started to rub my chest with quick circular motions. His head remained on my shoulder and his breath in my ear; he was puffing hard. As his hand started to rub my tummy Master Gahil coughed loudly and the uncle released me.

The third uncle was short and thin. He walked toward me from around the other side of the table. Although he was ugly, he had a nice smile. He said gently, 'Little princess, that song was lovely. I would love to hear you sing for me later; would you do that?' I hesitated, looked around the table, and nodded. 'Come here . . . to Uncle Nir,' he said. I inched toward him and as I did so he smiled sweetly. I came to his arms and he held me close. I turned my head against his belly and felt his tummy rising up and down quite fast. He was wearing a light brown suit and a white shirt. He was clean and his shoes were shiny. Uncle Smiley-Nir then released me and said, 'Go say hello to your next uncle.'

The previous uncles had been quite old (about the age of Master Gahil or Father) but this uncle was young. As he walked toward me I could see that his face was sweating. He was a small man, thin, and in a gray suit. He did not hug me at all but extended his hand toward me. I was not sure what to do until Master Gahil said, 'Take his hand in yours, princess.' I extended my two hands to his one. It was funny in a way because my hands were shaking and his hand was shaking and we both had to concentrate hard for them to meet. I took his trembling outstretched hand in my two hands. My little hands were small against his and I thought he had big hands for a little man. His hand was moist between mine. The uncle said in a quiet voice that trembled like his hand, 'I too enjoyed your singing . . . can you give Uncle a little kiss just here?' He pointed to his cheek as he leaned down toward me. I gave him a little kiss on his cheek and felt his wet lips on mine.

Master Gahil's booming voice interrupted, 'All right, gentlemen, let's take our seats,' and the sweaty little uncle stepped away from me and sat down. The master ordered, 'Princess, come here, darling, and stand next to me.' I obeyed; there was something about him that made you obey. As I stood next to him, he put his hand around my waist and continued, 'Gentlemen, I think it obvious that this is a jewel. I have not in many, many years seen such a lovely little fledgling.' The fat smelly uncle interrupted him and addressed a question to the old woman. 'Is she clean . . . has the doctor checked her?' The old woman answered from the shadows at the back of the room, 'Dr. Dasdaheer gave her a thorough examination earlier today. I have his report here. He says that she is in perfect health and,' she coughed, 'pure.' Fat Uncle and Young Big-handed Uncle both grunted together like hungry hogs.

Master Gahil, with his arm still around my waist, continued. 'Gentlemen, it is time for business. Who is going to enjoy our little princess fresh from the country?' He looked around, eyeing each uncle before continuing. 'Let's start, say, at fifty thousand rupees.' The cushion of silence was brief as Fat Uncle and Young Big-handed Uncle both spoke together. 'I'll go there' and 'Sure,' they

67

said simultaneously. Master Gahil said, 'Seventy-five thousand?' looking around the table; Tall Uncle, Uncle Smiley-Nir, and Fat Uncle all assented with nodding grunts. The master continued, 'A hundred thousand, one lakh.' I had been to livestock auctions with Father and my brothers and realized that I now was attending the same. There were more grunts of agreement and then Uncle Smiley-Nir interrupted and asked me, 'Darling, did any of your brothers or cousins or uncles ever touch you between the legs or put any toy or perhaps themselves between your legs?' I had no idea what he was talking about and shook my head. Uncle Smiley-Nir then looked at Master Gahil and said quietly, with the same smile on his face, 'Gahil, let me make this quick, as our little princess is tiring fast. Will anyone here go over five lakh . . . cash?' There was not even the sound of breathing. I heard the old woman's clothes rustle in the hush.

Master Gahil said, 'Gentlemen? Do I hear any advance?' He waited, but the hogs' grunting had ceased. Master Gahil exclaimed flamboyantly, 'Going, going, going . . . gone.' He was grinning so excessively from ear to ear that I thought the top of his head would flop off. Then he spoke. 'Nir, she is yours.'

Uncle Smiley-Nir then turned to me and

said, 'Darling, I so look forward to hearing more of your singing. I will be with you in just a minute.' The old woman drifted toward me from the dark, took my still-trembling hand, and led me from the room. As I left, I turned to see Uncle Smiley-Nir dealing bank notes to Master Gahil.

~

It is well known that the crane[1] stands dead still in the shallow water. I used to watch the cranes for hours with Grandpa. We would sit next to each other by the river, never touching and never talking. There was no old-man gibberish or child gibberish. We would sit and share the silence together. He taught me that the crane can feel when the fish approach by the change in water flowing against its legs. Grandpa was wrong but I never told him so.

The crane never knows when fish are approaching; it is simply always ready. The crane bends its body at its hips so that its eyes stare down into the water, and thereafter it

---

[1] The word used in the original notebook is the Hindi *bandhura*, बन्धुरा. It has a double meaning: both 'crane' and 'prostitute.'

stands still as steel, poised. At the moment the crane sees a fish within its reach, *bam!* It throws its beak into the water. The closed beak pierces the water and opens under it to grab the fish. Once the beak closes over the fish, the crane lets its neck go floppy, allowing the fish some freedom to wriggle. The crane uses the fish's own momentum to draw it from the beak cavity into its throat. It is a dance of one second but if you watch many such motions you will see this. The crane fishes in exactly the same way regardless of whether it is hot or the monsoon rains are falling. It is constant in variable surroundings.

Little girls are not cranes. They never stand still; they run inside when the weather darkens and it rains. There were bars across my window and a lock on my door and the clouds were very dark. I could feel the flow of water changing beneath me, but I did not have the ability to remain constant in the shifting stream.

~

The old woman led me back to my room. I was still overcome by the smells of the dining room and by the experience of meeting my new uncles. I felt emotionally layered, like a hut painted in many colors, one on top of the next: tiredness superseded by loneliness, coated in panic. I did not cry for fear of ruining my makeup.

Again I was locked alone in the room. Candles burned from tall black metal candelabras that had been placed on both sides of the bed. I jumped onto the bed as if it were an island that would enable me to avoid the swirling undercurrent beneath me. The bed had been made up with fresh crisp white sheets that shone in the candlelight, making the bed appear to me as a glowing refuge, fool that I was.

Minutes later the old woman returned with a tray on which lay a plate of sweet-cakes, but I had lost my taste for them. I was hungry, though, but more for Mother's stew. Also on the tray were incense sticks, which the old woman lit. They were not as gagging as the ones in the dining room but I still detested the smell. Grandma, who never threw away anything, used to overspice the meat to hide the fact that it was partially rotten. Her spices did not hide the meat's taste and the incense sticks did not disguise the doom that hung in the air.

The old woman sat down in the chair next to the bed. I looked at her but she did not look at me. I could sense a tension in her. She continued to stare downward at nothing. I was comfortable in the silence but asked, 'Can I have my coloring things?' She glanced up at me, moving only her eyes. Her only answer was a pencil-thin smile that skimmed across her mouth.

There was a soft knock at the door. The old woman unhurriedly got up and opened it and in walked Uncle Smiley-Nir. 'Hello there,' he chimed, with his big smile stuck on his face. He looked at me on the bed as if I were a precious vase. 'It's Batuk . . . right? Remember me? I'm Uncle Nir.' I looked down at the floor and nodded. 'Batuk,' he continued, in a slow, carefully metered voice, 'we are going to have a lovely time together. But first, my little darling, I want to hear you sing some more.' I nodded and said, 'Yes, Uncle.' I looked at the floor and noticed a centipede inching toward the bed, looking for sanctuary there. The old woman stood up and drifted to the far end of the room next to the door (in case I tried to escape?). Uncle Nir took his place, sitting with his hands on his knees on the wooden chair next to the bed. He smiled at me.

Then Uncle Nir got up from the chair and perched on the edge of the bed. 'Now, let me hear you sing again,' he said. His tone was no longer gentle. I could not remember the words to any song and I felt tears starting to fill my eyes, but I still did not cry. The old woman coughed and I knew she was about to reprimand me when 'Goat Song' somehow popped into my head.

I started to sing in a small voice and with little enthusiasm but I saw that Uncle Smiley-Nir was enraptured with me. He maintained his unceasing close-lipped grin that showed pleasure and nodded at me encouragingly. As I have written, he was physically ugly; it was not that he had three eyes and two noses, but rather that the two eyes and one nose that he did have did not quite fit on his face. Also, his face was too big for his neck. There was just something not-fitting about him; all of him was the wrong size. He continued to smile and nod but then he took off his shiny shoes. I sang,

Goat — goat — try and run
Over the hills and far away

There are birds in the air
Where you go — they will say

Goat — goat — try and run
Over the hills and far away

There are fish in the stream
Where you drink, I will know

Goat — goat — try and run
Over the hills and far away

There are blades of grass
Where you eat, they will tell

Goat — goat — try and run
Over the hills and far away.

After I finished the song, he clapped his little manicured hands and broadened his smile. 'Batuk, that was lovely. Now would you stand up and sing that again for me . . . would you . . . please?' I did not move and the nighttime noises of the street seemed to become louder in the silence. The smile fell from his face and he repeated, 'Stand up and sing, Batuk.' His voice was quiet but in my mind, I trembled. Disobedience was not an option.

I stood up on the bed and sang the song again. On the last chorus my voice faltered. When I finished the song he looked up at me, smiling. 'Now, there's nothing to be scared of. Come over here and sit on Uncle's lap.' I hoped that what he had just said would disappear if I ignored it (I used to handle demands from Mother in the same way). But the command hung in the air and I took three steps uneasily across the bed and lowered myself onto Uncle Nir's lap. My legs lay against his, dangling over the side of the bed. He folded his arms around my body and pulled my back close against his chest. He was breathing through my hair. Tears started to roll down my face and fall onto my lovely sari. His hands loosened their grip and he started to massage the sides of my chest with his hands, up and down like polishing furniture. He whispered in my ear, 'You see, there's nothing to cry about, I'm as gentle as a pussycat.' I could feel the warmth of his breath. 'You sing so beautifully.' He slid both his hands to the front of my chest and continued rubbing up and down. He started to rub the top and sides of my thighs. I was paralyzed. As he rubbed, horror washed through me.

Under his touch I blackened, like a pot of ink being poured over paper. The blackness soaked across, through, and inside me. Go on, touch me! Now take your hands from my skin and look. Look! You can see the ink stain. Go ahead, try to wash me off. No, you will need far more water than that; I am forever in the creases of your fingertips.

I scream and claw and kick against him. The old woman comes over to restrain me. She grasps my wrists and pins me down; she is one strong goat. He grabs my kicking ankles (I landed a few blows on his crowlike chest), spreads my legs apart, and sinks his body between them. I cannot kick him off. From her pocket, the old woman draws strands of white cotton with which she ties my wrists together and straps them to the back of the bed. Another wad of cotton is pushed in my mouth to stop the screaming and the biting. I try to bite her fingers as she pushes the cotton in. It almost chokes me and I gag. The old woman slaps me hard across the face. Uncle Nir grins and says, 'Oh, you're a strong little thing. This is more fun than I'd hoped.' I keep throwing my head, as it is the only thing I have left to defy him with. The old woman swats me again and again across the face with her bony hand until Uncle says, 'That's all right . . . I've got her. Now let's see what she's really made of.'

A moment of silence lapses. Looking down at me, his eyes glistening, he penetrates. Seconds later I feel his hot black ink gush from him and pulse into Bunny Rabbit's mouth. It sweeps through me — I can feel it; his blackness courses through me.

I take my eyes and turn them around to look inside myself. It is like seeing a wave crash onto the riverbank. The black torrents wash within me and I watch my light darken. I have used up so much energy in the fight that I have no resistance. I can see waves of black cascading through me in streams. I can see pools of darkness forming. I look for somewhere to hide but there is nowhere. I look in my kidneys, black. I travel to my tummy, black. My head too is black. I spring to my legs — useless legs that failed me — those stupid paralyzed sticks — they are black. I zip across to my hands — yes, they clawed, but that is just another embrace — black. My pounding heart pumps the blackness deeper within me, carried by every corpuscle. He has left nowhere for me to go. Everywhere I seek, every nook and avenue is awash with darkness. But then I see my salvation.

All words are hewn from black. When you take all the words written in the world and push them together in a cup, what do you get? A cup filled with blackness from which the words ascend and descend. We may think that a word is our own as we hear it or write it, but no, the words are on loan. Words can be young and bouncing like children and they can age like people. Like dead people, words ultimately return to the black from where they came.

And so I look within myself and assemble myself in words. I take the words that are my thoughts and dreams and hide them behind the dark shadow of my kidney. I compress my need for love into words and hide that as a drop of blackness next to my liver (it will be safe there until I need it). I transcribe the poetry of life into words, and with care slide it between sinews of muscle where he will not find it. I craft the words of merriment and sadness (they are the same) into a pyramid and place it under my skin so I can touch it whenever I need to know where my feelings are. I compile my memories into a record full of words and slip that into a slot left open for it in my head. There is plenty of room for all the words in the world to live in me; they are welcome here. He may have taken my light and extinguished it, but now within me can hide an army of whispering syllables, rhythms, and sounds. All you may see is a black cavity that fills a tiny girl, but trust me, the words are there, alive and fine.

The time for sweet smiles and placating words is over. He pushes off me. There is a gray tinge to his skin and not a hint of that smile. I have scratched his face and back. He has blood (mine?) on his thighs. His issue is inside me, sliding down my left thigh. Street air caresses my body and cools the sweat he has left on me. I close my eyes, still bound in white cotton restraints, and tell my power to take his soul and kill him.

He stands and takes the towel that is offered to him by the old woman. He walks from the bedroom with the white towel wrapped around his hips. Although neither he nor the old woman can see it, he also wears a dense, heavy maroon cloak that hangs from his shoulders. When he was a little boy, he bore this cloak, given to him by his parents, with ease. Now that he is a failed man, he can only just move under its weight. The brilliance of all light is blocked from him so that he will live in darkness forever.

~

I lay completely motionless. I could not move and I did not think. I felt no pain or sadness, just exhaustion.

The old woman returned after a few minutes and said, 'You cannot bathe yet because your uncle is still in there. But when he is done you can bathe, and then you will sleep.' She pulled the gag out of my mouth and untied my wrists. There was a sting where the wrist-ties were but I could feel nothing else. She sat in the wooden chair next to my bed.

I said nothing. I did not move because I refused to order my stupid legs to do anything. Then the old woman touched my hair. I pulled away only out of surprise. I heard again the noises from the street and listened intently to them as if they were music. I had no real sense of time and my tears had long stopped falling. I did not think of Mother and Father and I did not think of home. I thought intently of nothing. After a time I raised my eyes to the old woman. I stared at her, and for a second she was beautiful to me. Only for a second, though. She stared blankly out the window, unaware of my gaze. Tears rolled down her cheeks one by one. She showed no expression and did not utter any noise. She stared out the window and silently cried. She did not try to touch me again.

A time passed and the gentle rumble of the late-night traffic was eventually interrupted by the old woman. 'Get up now; you have to wash.' I tried to get onto my legs. The sari and my underclothes had long been ripped from me and I stood naked on the floor. The old woman gave me a white towel. I set my legs far apart because I did not trust them and I was in pain. I staggered slowly toward the washroom behind the old woman. I did not notice the blood dripping from my rabbit's mouth that left a trail behind me.

The room with the bathtub smelled of

steam and the floor was wet. I climbed into the empty bathtub and noticed that it was still warm from the previous user. I looked down and saw a tiny pool of blood forming between my legs on the floor of the white bathtub. Both the old woman and I stared at it but neither of us reacted; we just watched as the puddle grew bigger. The old woman turned on the water and the little puddle floated away, leaving only the faintest remnant of red on the bathtub floor as it filled with water.

I soaked in the hot water for a while. The old woman did not hurry me, clean me, or speak to me, and there were no scented oils this time. I climbed out of the tub with considerable difficulty, as my strength was drained. The old woman wrapped me in my towel and we returned to the bedroom. I could see that the drips of blood had stained the stone floor.

I fell onto the bed and crawled upward to the pillow. The old woman locked the door as she left. I would never see her again.

The windows were open and I could smell the street. I was lucky that the man did not touch my pillow. My head sank into it. All that I could smell as I fell asleep was the bleach that was used to wash the pillow white.

~

Not too busy a day. Puneet, clad in a bandage from his waist to his thigh, is still gloomy. I have become used to Puneet parading his made-up, dressed-sexy beauty at the gateway to his nest, and I miss it. It was my daily theater. He would flaunt himself at the entrance of his nest in his tight little shorts, brassiere, top, and chiffon veil, and I would watch him tilt his upper body a trace to accentuate his bottom. I would see him straighten a curl and toss the edge of the veil to cast a web of air to draw men to him — like a fisherman throwing his net on the river. The fact that he was a boy only pronounced his femininity. There were many times when I was sure my simple, chin-down, eyes-up fluttering smile would entice a novice cook (the most valuable) toward me only for him to become entrapped in Puneet's deviant, honey-kissed web. To put it simply, there were many men who never dreamed of lying upon the throne of a boy whom Puneet persuaded otherwise. He would tell me, often with a salacious grin, that when they felt his mouth on theirs, he became woven into their dreams. He said that their tongues would first press hesitantly against his, but then would dance and weave with his. His theory was that all men had a part of him inside them; it was just waiting to be released. His constant river of business attested to this.

Despite Puneet's gloominess, men still stood waiting in the Common Street until the moment his curtain opened. Oftentimes, as soon as one devotee left him, I would see a man accelerate or even trot from halfway down the street to ensure he reached Prince Puneet's gate before any other. Even when Puneet just plopped himself outside his door and did not advertise his promise, men would drift to him. It could be that his sultriness intensified his attractiveness. A forbidden pleasure unadvertised is perhaps the sweetest.

I tried to think back to the village. For sure all the boys wanted the toy that other boys had. However, there was also the toy that was too dangerous to play with, which had a unique allure. Jitendra was my age and the weakest and smallest of the boys. Not only was he physically slight, but he also was an insignificant person who was annoying at every opportunity. He was like a small pebble stuck in your shoe. All the boys and even several of the girls would pick on him; you could blow and he would crumble. He was friendless. However, this all changed when he received a flick-knife for his birthday, sent to him by a stupid uncle from Delhi. If you pressed a button on the knife's handle, the blade shot out. The blade's edge was jagged and so sharp that it could slice a rat's head clean off. This became a favored trick of Jitendra's.

Walking through the village one day, a ten-year-old boy, a year or so older than Jitendra, tried to take the knife from him. In the struggle, Jitendra pressed the button and the blade shot out into the boy's flank; cascades of blood poured forth and torrential screaming. That night frightful rows broke out between the parents, and both boys were severely punished. However, after the thigh-slicing incident Jitendra was never picked on again, although he remained friendless. He became feared by the village children as well as by the local rats. There are 'toys' that require a certain courage to possess and thereby acquire a special attraction. Jitendra's knife was one such toy. Puneet was another.

Puneet had been a 'lost boy' from the time his mother disappeared. The fact that he survived is a miracle. He has told me of atrocities he has seen on the street even before Master Gahil acquired him: murders, tortures, and violent robberies to name a few. He told me how his father broke out of prison to try to find him, only to be recaptured after a sensational street battle. He explains frequently how his mother married a wealthy businessman who will fetch him, 'any day now — just you watch.' The stories about his parents are fiction. Puneet has long been erased from the memories of his father and mother. How else could they reconcile their place on earth, knowing that their son lives two nests down from mine and every day pleasures men who are filthy inside and out? Puneet has no reality other than his cage and this street. That is why he never seeks to escape; this is all there is.

~

Puneet slides inside his nest, following a man in an ill-fitting gray suit. Puneet's body speaks to his latest round of defeat, although his eye and lip makeup are still meticulously applied. He is becoming thin and his bandages slide down his waist, even without him bending over to display his love-hole. I have a great idea to cheer him up; I will write him a story. It does not matter that he cannot read; I will read it to him. In point of fact, I am the only person I know who can read.

Dear my beloved Puneet, this story is for you. I hope you love it.

THE GRAIN OF RICE

The Master taught, 'The world balances on a grain of rice.'

The students asked the Master, 'Master, how can the whole world, with all the elephants, houses, cities, palaces, crops, fields, and sky, balance on a grain of rice?'

The Master smiled serenely, looked over the field of students before him, and told this tale.

In a distant kingdom was a small village, and in that small village lived a family, a farmer, his wife, and their five children, two girls and three boys. The youngest of the boys was strong, quick-witted, and agile but beyond these traits he was connected to the flow of the earth. In his previous lives he had been the horse that was ridden by the greatest of all kings, a tiger that had given his coat to a queen, and a prince who was destined to rule the greatest kingdom on earth, except that he was cut down by jealousy. Now, in this life, he was born as the youngest son of a poor farmer. But how his inner beauty shone. Even as a little boy his radiance drew attention from seers and the blind alike. Rumors spread of a holy child gifted with inner sight and the power to heal.

To look at this fourteen-year-old boy, you might be distracted by his physical beauty. He was blossoming into manhood and his lean and muscular body could twist with a change in the wind. His eyes were entrancing and his face lovely to behold. But if you were able to look beyond this shell of physical beauty, you would see something even more glorious. He shone with the wisdom of eternity, for he could see not only this life and the last but also the next. He could see the false pride of the rich and the faked lament of the poor. He could separate love from lust and could taste spring in the air even when it was winter. His name was Puneet.

In the village, the crops had failed for the third year in a row and the earth was barren. The stream that had fed the village no longer ran and the drinking wells were almost completely dry. The village had long used up all its reserves of food and the villagers were starving in the streets. The farmer said to his youngest son early one morning, 'Darling Puneet, we are all starving. You are a very special boy with tremendous powers. You must leave the village and seek fortune for us.

87

Bring us back riches so that we may buy food and eat.' Within the hour, before the ferocity of the morning sun took hold, Puneet bade farewell to his father, mother, and brothers and sisters. He gathered up some pebbles, wrapped them in a rag, and slung them over his shoulder, heading out from the village on foot.

He walked for many days through unimaginable heat and evaded many dangers. He found water by following animal tracks and ate roots and plants that had grown on the side of the path to sustain him. He came to a large town. By then he was dusty and very thin but he still carried the pebbles from his village. This was a rich town full of greed and falseness. At the town inn, he drank from the trough used by the horses until his thirst was satisfied. He scavenged in the garbage of the inn for food, of which there was plenty. He ate until his strength returned. Wandering through the village, he saw how the poor and rich coexisted, neither sharing grace with the other, and he saw falsehood and greed all around him. He vomited the food he had eaten, for he did not want the filth of this town inside him.

At the village square, he beheld a great commotion. Since he was slender, he easily slid his way to the front of the crowd, which had gathered around a wrestling ring built upon a wooden platform. The ring was square and bounded by ropes. In the middle of the ring stood a giant. He was taller than an elephant and almost as broad. The shadow he cast from the sun almost filled the ring. In front of the giant kneeled a bloodied man, his armor half cut from him; he was begging for mercy from the giant. The giant looked across at a beautiful woman who sat on a throne at the far end of the ring, and the crowd hushed. She was the queen of the mighty kingdom; she wore a golden crown studded with a multitude of pearls and diamonds and a glistening golden cloak draped over her shoulders. Her hair was oiled and she appeared as a vision in a famous painting. To her right and left sat two lions with chains around their necks thicker than a man's arm, and at her feet was a chest of gold coins.

She spoke into the silence. 'Let him live, but for failing the challenge, he, his wife, and his children shall become my slaves. Soldier, do you accept these terms?' The groveling man had dried blood on his face and fresh blood oozing from his wounds. He answered, 'Beloved queen, I and my family would be honored beyond measure to be your servants for eternity.' With that, the queen waved her hand to silence the murmuring crowd. 'Kill him, giant,' she ordered, 'and have his family burned alive in the foundry. A man whose family is so easily bought is a family not worth having — even as slaves. A man with so little honor is not worthy to drink even the water of my kingdom. We must purge the realm of such weakness. Kill him now! That is my command.'

The giant, with one swoop of his massive sword, severed the soldier's head from his body. Blood shot out from the soldier's neck, splattering over a village woman who was standing beside the ring. The queen silenced the astonished crowd. 'Quiet!' she shouted. 'Are there any other heroes in this town who wish to earn this chest of gold by killing my giant?' There was silence.

Meanwhile, the giant had taken out a short knife from his hip and was kneeling beside the dead soldier. He proceeded to cut the heart from the lifeless body. Holding the dripping organ in his hand, he smeared it across his chest so that it blended with the dried blood from previous challengers. He stood up and roared and raised the dismembered heart above his head in his blood-smeared fist. A huge cheer rose from the crowd. And then Puneet stepped into the ring.

There was immediate silence, broken by a thunderous laugh from the giant. 'What, boy? Are you the sacrificial lamb?' The queen waved her hand and spoke to Puneet. 'Boy, what are you doing in the ring? Is this bloody carcass your father? Are you here to avenge him?' Puneet answered the queen, 'No, mighty queen. I am not his son. I am here to earn the chest of gold.' The queen laughed and said, 'Do you not know that to earn this chest of gold, you have to kill my giant? He has hacked the heart out of a hundred men twice your size.' Puneet answered, 'Most noble queen, I accept your challenge, but I ask one favor of you since I am not armed.' 'Ask,' said the queen. Two street dogs had entered the ring and were grazing on the soldier's heartless carcass. Puneet said to the queen, 'May I please borrow from you one gold coin? If I win the challenge, it will be mine, and if I lose it, you may take it from my dead hand.' The queen asked, 'What do you have to offer as collateral?' She was amused by the beautiful boy, whom she rather fancied for her own plaything. 'This,' Puneet answered, holding up the bag of pebbles from his town. 'It is some pebbles from my town.' The queen burst out laughing, along with the crowd. 'For the sake of sport,' said the queen, 'I accept your terms. Loan him one gold coin.'

Puneet carefully placed the bag of pebbles on the floor of the wooden ring in front of the queen and he received a single gold coin from one of the queen's attendants. The remains of the soldier were dragged off and the ring was cleared. There was absolute silence as the small boy faced the giant. The giant growled in a voice that resembled thunder, 'You are not even a snack for me. You are not even a mouthful.' Puneet responded, 'Mighty warrior, I cannot fight you.' There were jeers from the crowd. The queen waved for silence. She was angered, for she enjoyed watching men dismembered before her. 'Boy, you agreed to fight. You have no choice.' Puneet answered, 'It is not that I am afraid to fight, Your Highness. It is that your beauty is so overpowering that I cannot fight while you are within my sight.' The queen loved flattery, as all vain people do, and she smiled. 'I cannot make myself less beautiful,' she said. Puneet answered, 'Your Majesty, even if you were half as beautiful, your beauty would still blind even the keenest eye.' 'What do you suggest?' asked the queen, who was enjoying this public exchange. The giant, on the other hand, was becoming irritable, as he was eager for his snack. Puneet continued, 'May I ask that the giant stand between me and you, so that I may fight bravely without your beauty blinding me?' The queen laughed and felt a woman's desire for this beautiful young man. 'Let it be so.' The boy and the giant switched positions and faced each other. The town square hushed to a painful silence. You could hear the buzz of the summer heat that scorched the back of Puneet's neck.

'Fight now!' roared the giant, and stomped toward him. Puneet watched as the giant's massive feet thumped on the wooden platform, approaching him step by step. Puneet waited without moving a muscle as the giant advanced. The moment that Puneet smelled the giant's fetid breath, he spun the gold coin high in the air. The giant looked upward at the shining, spinning coin. As he did so, he was blinded for a moment by the sunlight that reflected off the coin, for this is why Puneet had switched fighting positions. Puneet, who knew the cycle of all life, understood that if the whole world balances upon a grain of rice, then so does a giant. As the giant was blinded by the coin, he lost his balance. Puneet sprang forward and pushed on the giant's right knee with all his might. The giant wobbled and toppled backward, spinning his arms round and round as he fell. He landed on the wooden platform with such force that he shook the entire earth. The giant's mighty head was the last part of his body to hit the platform, and when it did, it landed right on top of Puneet's little bag of pebbles. The giant's head split open like a melon and his brain spilled onto the ring's floor like lassi. He was dead before the gold coin landed on the wooden ring.

There was stunned silence and then the town square erupted in screaming cheers.

'You see, my beloved students, the world is balanced upon a grain of rice.' Then the Master was silent.

The students, sitting in their orange robes, were taken aback by the story, for it was a very strange tale indeed. After a while, one student raised his hand and asked, 'Honored Master, did Puneet then take the gold back to his village? Did he marry the queen and become the greatest ruler on earth as was his destiny?'

The great Master smiled. 'No. It did not end like that.' The Master enjoyed a little silence before continuing. 'After the giant fell, Puneet immediately grabbed the gigantic sword from the giant's dead hand and thrust it straight through the neck of the queen.

'You see, my students, a queen who sells the death of her subjects for sport is not a queen. Her death was married to the death of the fallen soldier.'

Another student asked, 'But what of Puneet's family . . . what of the starving village, dear Master?'

The great Master looked into nothingness and answered, 'After watching the queen die, Puneet closed his eyes and listened to the screams of his father and his mother and his brothers and his sisters and of the villagers crying for food. He could hear the cries of agony that are special for those dying of starvation. Puneet pushed his mind deeper, pushed aside his heart, and willed their deaths.'

There was a gasp from the students. One asked, 'But how can that be, oh great Master?'

The Master waited for his students to settle their inner commotion so that they could listen. He waited with them for two days before answering. Eventually he said, 'What village loses three years of crops and does not either find new water or relocate to the valley? What father sends forth his son to save him? Puneet rose to the upper air and willed them all to die, for they had willed death upon themselves.'

The oldest of the students sat in the front row. He loved and was beloved of his Master. He asked, 'Beloved Master. What is it that you will of us?' The Master, who was the greatest of the great teachers and who was once a boy who had felled a giant with a single gold coin, answered, 'To have no will at all.'

The end. Love, Batuk.

~

I learned to read and write at the missionary's medical clinic, where I was sent when I was seven. The illness that landed me there was entirely my mother's fault, at least according to Grandma.

As a little girl, I would find any excuse to go to the river, whether to fish with Grandpa, or play, or even wash clothes. I could always be found on the riverbank. It was strange because unlike my friends I hated to get wet! I liked to be next to the river, though. I was entranced by the music of the water and the dance that light played on it. I liked the sense of loneliness without being alone, for the water connected me to all life. I appreciate many years later that the Common Street is a river too; back and forth people flow, and containers, cars, and small buses. The flow never ceases to connect the world to me, to take me to it.

On the day in question — the air was wet and yet the sky a cloudless blue — I returned from the river in the early evening. As soon as I walked through the hut's entrance and coughed, Grandma said to Mother, 'I tell you not to let her sit by the river all the time. Now look at her, she's sick.'

Grandma had the extraordinary gift of making even a simple phrase sound like a tirade of disapproval directed toward my mother. For example, Grandma could say, 'Pass the cake,' to which Mother would immediately respond, 'What's wrong with it?' Even if Grandma said, 'Oh, nothing,' her words conveyed that Mother's cake was no better than a mound of rotting flesh covered in icing. Grandma was very gifted in this regard. And so when Grandma directly accused Mother of deliberately trying to make me ill, Mother took the bait (as she always did). She spun round and snapped to Grandma, 'I told Batuk not to sit by the river all day, but you know what she's like, watching the lizards and talking to the grass. She is a fool, that one.' I coughed again but this time a little harder (I said that I have a taste for drama). 'There, I told you!' Grandma said. 'She isn't a fool. She's just simple. I would keep her on a rope.' I almost spoke back but let Grandma continue as I knew there was more fun to come. I was right. Grandma now turned up the volume and the shrillness of her voice box. 'You are the idiot!' Grandma squealed at Mother. 'You let her sit out all day — now look at her. Tell me, did I ever try to kill *you*? If I had treated you like you treat that little Batukee' — her pet name for me, which I loathed — 'my mother would have beaten me with a stick.'

This was terrific sport, so I threw in a coughing fit that lasted a full minute (the drama of the sick). Grandma threw me a momentary glance of pity (or was it applause?) and angled the edges of her mouth downward in preparation for the kill. 'If she dies,' spat Grandma, 'you will rot in prison on your fat behind and guess who will have to take care of the rest of those dear children . . . and that poor spastic Navaj?' Grandma often claimed that Navaj was handicapped because Mother had refused to drink Grandma's special pregnancy tea. I thought I had better cough some more (curtain rises on the second act). Grandma, with venom seeping from her skin, continued, 'I have already raised my family. Do you really think me strong enough to raise your family too? . . . Mind you . . . at least the children would survive through high school.' I then let rip the harshest cough a seven-year-old could muster. Grandma turned toward me with a mixture of pity and sheer delight in her eyes; I think she would only have been happier if I had dropped dead then and there. I watched the pity melt off her like butter in midday heat. She whipped her ever-intensifying glare back on Mother, took in a breath, and proclaimed, 'She needs the doctor' (cough), 'NOW!' (cough, cough). The odd thing was, I was actually extremely ill.

To her credit, Mother had learned well over the years. She simply deflected this shower of abuse at Father. Up until now Father had been silent, as he had been enjoying every second of the show. Mother screamed at him, 'You heard her, you good-for-nothing drunk, get her to the doctor.'

~

There were three ways to get medical attention. One way was to send a message to the neighboring town for the doctor to come to us, but we could never afford this. Another way was to have Father gather whatever money he could, load me onto a cart pulled by the field ox, and off we would head to the town a few hours away where the doctor resided. When we eventually arrived there, we would trek to the doctor's house and wait an eternity before I was seen. The doctor's consultation would last for moments before he pushed up his glasses and scribbled like an imbecile on a pad of paper. He would give his little drawing to the nurse, who subsequently would give Father a powder wrapped in a light, shiny brown paper sachet. The visit would conclude in a shouting match in which Father would explain that he had no more money 'than this' and the nurse would insist that he'd better find some.

The third way to receive a medical cure was to head to the neighboring town just as I described but not actually go to the doctor. Father would take me out for a sherbet and then leave me on the ox-drawn cart at the market square for an hour while he visited his cousin. Once he returned, with his cousin's lavender perfume on his shirt, we would head home, both of us happy. The sherbet must have contained some potent ingredients because I generally got better.

This occasion fell in the third category. I had a bright red sherbet and Father had tea. He tied the ox and cart up in the market square and left me there while he went to see his cousin. An hour later we started home, but now I really was coughing hard and by the time we got home I had a fever. Mother asked what the doctor said and Father lied that he had promised I would soon be well; we just had to ride out the fever with cool soaks. Mother asked Father if I had been given medicine and he explained that I had been and that I had already taken it. He then inserted an elegant detail to add authenticity to his lie by explaining that the powder was a white-brown mixture that smelled awful. I was too sick by then to confirm or deny his fiction.

I remained with a high fever for days and coughed up platefuls of yellow-and-brown slime that was sometimes bloodstained. The fevers climbed higher still and I stopped eating; the cough was unrelenting. I cried whenever I had the strength. People from the village came by to offer best wishes, diagnoses, and cures. The only thing that they all agreed upon was that the doctor we had gone to was a quack and a charlatan. I heard at least three people say he wasn't even a doctor. Father looked ashen.

After five days of ever-mounting fevers and a worsening cough, it was decided to take me to the missionary's medical clinic, which was a full day's ride away in Bhopal. I was bundled up and Father and I headed off before the sun had risen. We rode in the covered wagon pulled by the ox, and I was hacking all the way. When we arrived at the clinic, which was located on the outskirts of the city, the nurse listened to my father's story and saw me cough up what looked like berry-stained ghee. Much to my bemusement she collected a sample of this gunk as if it were a prize. When she returned a few hours later, she told Father that I had TB and needed to be admitted to 'the ward.' The ward was actually a large converted chicken hutch that now housed the sick. It smelled of its previous inhabitants, overlaid with the smell of iodine and illness. Along one wall of the ward were the women's beds and along the other, the men's. I was allocated a gray mattress and a steel bed about halfway down the women's wall. When Father left I was too sick to cry.

Despite my initial fear, I felt at ease, although I was the youngest patient by far. During the day, there was a constant stream of sound: wheels rolling; people groaning, vomiting, and dying; and the *buzz buzz* of flies and the whir of heat. At night, silence rested like a blanket over the snores and rustling of the forty-three patients and one nurse. I must have become numbed to the smell because I often saw visitors enter the ward and immediately rush out holding their mouths in disgust before choking and sometimes vomiting.

On the bed next to me lay a near-naked old woman who looked as though she were having a baby. She was far older than Grandma and so thin that her baby looked almost bigger than she did. One of her hands hung from the side of the bed; when her fingers moved I could see the sinews writhing through her skin, which was as thin and delicate as cigarette paper. Sometimes I would watch the gentle undulation of her pulse as she slept just to see if it ever stopped, and a few days later it did. Within an hour she was rolled on a tarpaulin and disappeared.

Lying on the bed on the other side of me was a woman about Mother's age who was twice as round as Mother. Her left foot was heavily bandaged and the nurses came by every day to change the dressings. Her foot had been cut off because it had gotten infected from sugar sickness. Oddly, she did not seem at all distraught that her foot lay in a waste bin somewhere. She seemed, in fact, to revel in the attention she received, as she was nearly always surrounded by people saying, 'You poor thing,' 'Tttt, it's a terrible disease,' 'You look wonderful' (albeit footless), and bringing her containers of the most fantastic food. The woman took pity on me from time to time and gave me some of the leftovers she had not scarfed down. But her acts of generosity were rare and she nearly always licked the containers of food clean. She left the clinic about two weeks after her operation, in a wooden box on wheels pushed by her rancid husband, who was always smoking. I bet she would have happily sacrificed the other foot for a few more weeks of pity and delicious food.

During the day, the ward was staffed by three nurses and a doctor. There were also two orderlies, who carried, mopped, cleaned, and when necessary removed those who died. There was also a priest. Every day, Father Matthew, a young, stringy white man, would talk to us for about half an hour and then give us each a piece of bread and fruit juice. He had a soft, lolling voice and a gentle manner that he tried to disguise when he addressed us each day. He would stand on the table in the middle of the ward by the entrance. As he talked, he gesticulated, shouted, and jumped up and down like a lunatic. This excessive exertion was unnecessary as none of us understood him and none of us were able to leave even if we wanted to. It was worth watching him, though, for the entertainment as well as for the bread and fruit juice. We were his forty-three-strong army of devotees, although all of us would later leave him, one way or another. Once or twice a day, he would walk along the two rows of beds and would always stop at mine, as I was the youngest. He would smile at me and I would smile at him. He carried his book and his cross, which I knew were important to him. I could tell that he often spoke to the nurses about me because I watched his eyes.

★ ★ ★

I did not have any visitors, which I was thankful for because I was learning to read.

After a week on the ward, I was feeling better but I was not allowed out of bed. The doctor, who led the daily parade of the medical staff, listened each day to my back with his rubber ears. Every day was the same; he would nod his head, mutter to the head nurse, write something on the board at the end of my bed, and move on — all without saying a word to me. The most junior of the nurses was called Hita. It was Hita who gave me reading.

Hita looked exactly like a girl from our village: she was healthy and round and had the loveliest smile (although she was missing several teeth). She would sit on my bed in her stiff white uniform and talk to me from time to time. One day, I asked her what the doctor was writing about me and she took the chart and read aloud, 'August seventh, making progress, keep on bed rest. Lung bases collapsed; consolidation in right mid zone. Allow food. No exercise.' 'He wrote all that on one line?' I asked. The scratches across the page fascinated me. She nodded. She bustled off and returned with a book, the cover of which showed a rabbit and a wheelbarrow, both of which were smiling. I opened the book and saw the patterns that the words made on the page. The shapes of the letters and the spaces that separated the words made the page look like a drawing. Nurse Hita showed me the first word and I repeated it. 'Rabbit.'[1] She left abruptly seconds later because a man on the other side of the room had inconveniently dislodged his pee tube and the liquid was pulsing onto the floor like beer from a toppled bottle. I stared at this word and repeated it over and over again, like a mantra.

---

[1] The word used in the original notebook is the Hindi śaśak, शशक.

Each day Hita, and in due course the other nurses, would teach me a word or two or three; I would spend the entire day reading my new words and practicing the ones I already knew. After a week I could read a paragraph. Hita was delighted with me. I explained to her that I wanted to read my book to the white man because he was always carrying a book with him and so I thought he must love to read too.

The late summer heat had let up and Father Matthew had become particularly expressive in his tabletop sermons. So much so that whenever he finished his incomprehensible ranting, which he always did with a dramatic flourish, those who had two hands applauded him while the handless cheered. I could see he was pleased with this reception. On one particularly cool evening, when Father Matthew arrived at my bed on his tour of the ward, Hita spoke to him in English. The Father then turned to me and gave me a nod and a welcoming smile. I had been rehearsing from sunrise and read the first two pages of my book to perfection. I even incorporated a little emotional expression into my reading, although I omitted gesticulations; the story was about a rabbit who helped cheer up his friend the wheelbarrow by helping him become more useful. When I finished reading, Father Matthew beamed and clapped his hands. After a moment's pause, he said something to Hita in English. The following afternoon a teacher came: Mr. Chophra, my own reading teacher.

Mr. Chophra came to teach me (and visit Hita) three times a week during the rest of my twelve-week stay on the ward. I was a fast study. Having walked across the desert with no water, I was thirsty and could not drink enough! Within three weeks I had rudimentary reading skills. Thereafter, Mr. Chophra brought books for me to read of advancing complexity. My thirst was not quenched, though, as I read the books almost as quickly as he brought them. I read from the great poets, stories of boys who went to the army, and even translations of some English books. Every day, Father Matthew would come and listen to me read. I knew that he did not understand me but this did not seem to matter. I understood that he too could hear the patterns that words made without the need to understand them. Each day that I read to him he beamed at me and applauded. After I finished, he would sit at the end of my bed and read to me from his special black book. He would read for five to ten minutes and I would sit back and listen to the rhythm of the words coupled to the softness of his voice. It sounded like a song. When he finished he would mark the page with a gold thread that was attached to the book's back. In this fashion we read to each other almost every day. I got into the habit of falling asleep at night reading a book and would wake up to the faint smell of book print and moldy pages.

I learned to write in concert with learning to read by hand-copying passages from the books Mr. Chophra gave me. It was obvious that Mr. Chophra was delighted to come and see me at every opportunity possible (even when I was fast asleep). It was not my thirst for reading that drew him to my bedside, however. It was Hita. On several occasions, I woke up from a nap and there Mr. Chophra was standing, gaily laughing with her. It was fun to watch them; he would blush and stumble and she would revel in his trepidation of her. After he left, she would often talk about him with the other nurses and they would collectively giggle as girls have a tendency to do. I once asked Hita if she liked Mr. Chophra. In response, she scolded me, and so I knew that she did. There was one occasion, when the ward was quiet, that Hita sat next to me throughout my entire lesson, staring like a hypnotized rabbit at her ever-smiling Chophra-barrow.

Mr. Chophra's ever-more-diverted attention

never bothered me, for whenever he came, under whatever pretext, he brought me more to read. The trouble was that I became so engrossed in my reading I forgot to pretend to be sick, and before I knew it, the silent doctor with the rubber ear pieces had written 'discharge' on the chart at the end of my bed.

On the day I was to leave, I dressed early in the day. I said goodbye to all of my fellow inmates and the staff; even the ever-silent doctor said, 'Goodbye and be well.' Mr. Chophra had come the evening before to give me a cardboard box full of books to read *and keep*. Just after the morning rounds, Father walked onto the ward. I was so excited to see him, I could not control myself. I sprinted across the ward, leaped into his arms, and hugged him. He grinned like a monkey, crying, 'Girl, you look so well. What have they been feeding you?' After the initial pleasantries we were at a loss as to what to say to each other and so I took him by the hand and gave him a tour of the ward, although I bypassed the patients who would probably die in the next day or two. Father Matthew had been fetched and came running onto the ward with the tails of his long black coat flying behind him. He shook my father's hand; the two giants were somewhat wary of each other but I willed their affection and it came to pass. Father

Matthew gave me my own Bible (Mother would later throw it away) and held me close to him for as long as it had taken me to read the opening paragraph of my first book many weeks before. I gave Father Matthew a poem I had been writing for several days. I had decorated the paper with trees and leopards and sunshine.

To Father Matthew:

Every day you come and read a little bit to me
Dressed in black, book in hand, happy I can see
I read to you a little bit. Not a word you understand
You listen hard, smile at me, and take me by the hand

You always pat my hand (twice); happy words you seem to say
I feel your hand holding mine, even when you've gone away

Love from Batuk.

After I read the poem and Hita translated it, he hugged me again and I could see that he wanted to cry. Hita, on the other hand, was sobbing. I looked at the little streams of water on her beautiful round face and hoped that she would see Mr. Chophra again.

~

On the long way home in the ox-drawn cart, I chatted inanely to Father, gesticulating with my arms as I spoke. Father was happy to listen to me with a quiet smile on his face. There were moments, though, when he would reach across the cart and touch my hair or accidentally bump me. Sometimes he would reach over and give me a little hug. Although he asked, I wouldn't tell him what was in the cardboard box.

When we stopped that night, we sat outside drinking tea and I made Father put his hat over his eyes. I took a book of stories from the top of the cardboard box and asked him if he was ready. I told him to keep his eyes closed, and I started to read to him. In the story the hero loses his beloved to another family. Her new husband treats her cruelly as he only married her for power and money and because he knows his wife loved another. The heartbroken wife escapes and tries to make her way back to the hero, who has been pining for her. On the return journey, by means of a river, a torrential storm sinks her boat and washes her up onto a tiny island in the middle of the river. The island begins to disappear as the waters rise, and she sends her cries of desperation into the winds. The hero hears her cries, dashes to a boat, and rides through the storm onto the island. Though his boat is also destroyed in the storm, he manages to clamber onto the island and rushes into her arms. The lovers die in each other's arms, and the island is submerged along with them.

Father did not say a word until I finished. As I concluded the story, I peeked under his hat; his eyes were shiny and tears were streaming down his face. He just stared at me. 'Father, there are happier stories, let me . . . ' 'Batuk, that is not why I am crying. I never imagined that any child of mine would ever learn to read . . . this is your ticket out of Dreepah-Jil.' He caught his thoughts and continued to speak excitedly. 'We will have to find you a teacher . . . One day you will be a . . . doctor, a lawyer.' I interrupted, 'Or a teacher.' 'Yes, darling, or a great teacher, Batuk. Come to me.' I went to my father with another book tucked under my arm, the magical abhang poems of Namdev. As I read words I barely understood and soaked them within me, my father held me. That night we both created dreams for me. Neither he nor I ever aspired to my becoming a prostitute.

~

Despite the story I wrote for him, Puneet remains miserable. Today, again, he sits at the entrance of his nest with his head down, moping. The bandages have gone (along with his bhunnas). I wave hello to him but really, I want to walk over and slap him across the face. I must admit that I think about him less and less these days. He waves back at me unenthusiastically. The good news is that he has more devotees than ever.

No one seems to mind that in between baking sessions, I sit at the entrance to my nest, my pad on my knees, writing. My earlier fear of my notepad being discovered was unfounded as Mamaki cannot read, although she is able to place check marks against our names in her little book. She quite likes that I 'scribble away' at the entrance to my nest because this seems to bring in cooks rather than deter them. Novice cooks will often walk up to me from the street and ask what I am writing. My answer is always the same: 'I'm just scribbling' (men don't like to feel stupid). My writing creates an easy way for shy men to approach me, and once they have done so, Mamaki pounces. She throws open her arms and swoops them under the folds of her sari, into my nest; job done! Also, with me sitting and scribbling, Mamaki can point down and talk about me to men who are walking by. She said to me yesterday (I am fast becoming her favored), 'Maybe I should get all the others to scribble too.'

For me, the cooks become my paragraph ends or, sometimes, my chapter breaks. The afternoons are often the quietest and that is when I generally write in my book. This afternoon is hot. I call to Puneet, 'Puneet, I have a joke for you!' Meera's little head pops out from the cage between ours with a big grin. 'Oh, I love jokes,' she says with a smile on her squished-up face. Puneet is unmoved and grunts. I continue, 'What do you call a dog with two heads?' Meera squawks, 'Woof, woof.' 'Other one, other one,' she pipes. 'All right,' I say, 'what do you call an elephant leaning against a tree?' Meera furrows her brow; she is adorable. I answer, 'Bruised.' Meera looks puzzled. 'I do not get it.' Puneet then speaks in a most gloomy drone. 'It's because the tree fell over and the elephant hurt itself.' (It is a terrible joke but I am awful at jokes.) Meera then responsively bursts into hoots of laughter and I laugh with her; she really is a child (this is her key selling point). Mamaki takes extra for her by telling her cooks that she is ten years old when in fact she is twelve. 'Other one, other one,' Meera calls. I think for a while and say in an undertone, 'What do you call a woman with three titties?' Meera shakes her head and shrugs. 'Mamaki Hippopotamus,' I answer, 'two on her chest and one on her chin.' Meera breaks into hysterics. Then Puneet perks up: 'What do you call a woman with a beard?' He sits up straight. Meera answers, 'Mamaki Hippopotamus.' 'Yes,' Puneet says a bit too loudly, and laughs for the first time in ages. I continue, 'Puneet, what happened to the sixth girl of our group?' Puneet answers, 'She is in between Mamaki's buttocks.' Meera is laughing so hard I think she will wet herself. Meera says, 'My go, my go,' barely able to get out the words. She says, 'Where is Mamaki's husband?' I answer, 'Between her titties.' No response. Meera and Puneet are silent and both are looking over my left shoulder. 'He's dead,' Mamaki says from behind me, and waddles off down the street. The three of us are silent for as long as we can possibly be, but then Puneet starts to smirk. His smirk becomes my giggle and soon

116

the three of us break out in floods of laughter. Gripping his stomach, Puneet, who is almost crying with laughter, says, 'He suffocated . . . they were having sex and he slipped inside her . . . That's why she walks like that.'

That was the last tummy-aching laugh we would ever share together.

~

I first met Puneet in what is referred to as the Orphanage. It covers a space about half the size of the meat market and is a series of bamboo poles that support a patchwork of threadbare cloths of many vintages. As one cloth piece becomes decrepit and falls apart, it is replaced with another piece that is slightly less worn.

The Orphanage is policed by Yazaks, men and women who have divested themselves of humanity. Yazaks view their orphans solely in terms of the income they provide. The Yazaks reside in a brick house at the easternmost end of the Orphanage, from which sounds of music and television continuously blare. Interestingly, except where money is concerned, the policing is lax because there are so many children who are indistinguishable

117

from each other. The Orphanage is made up of a herd of street urchins who reside there until called upon to perform some service or other, for which they are directly rewarded with food, clothing, or sometimes (rarely) money. No work, no food. No one steals from the Yazaks or cheats them because just as a child's presence is anonymous, so is his or her absence. Many rumors abound; for example, I heard about a child from the Orphanage who stole a bicycle on his own and pocketed twenty rupees from a fence without telling his Yazak. The fence told the Orphanage, as the child's wrist tattoo was a signature that identified him as coming from this particular Orphanage. Justice was immediate and occurred in the open. Using his right hand, the Yazak lifted the child, age eleven or twelve, by his hair off the ground and with his left hand cut his throat with a Damascus blade. Before the second spurt of blood had shot from his neck, the Yazak had thrown the boy to the ground just as you might throw away a sweets wrapper. Before the boy's soul was released at the moment of death a minute later, he had been stripped of his meager clothes and shoes by the other urchins. That evening another child collected a bowl of rice with sauce for carrying the body to the public dump, the burial ground of the poor.

The girls are not spared Yazak savagery. There was an instance where a girl had her vagina sewn shut for copulating for her own pleasure. This was done by a large female Yazak with a needle and thread while sitting on the girl, with older children restraining each limb. A hole was left for urination but this is generally irrelevant either because the girl manages to remove the stitches herself with a knife or broken glass, or infection sets in on the inevitable path to the garbage dump. For second offenders, the clitoris is sliced away and the vagina sewn completely shut; few second offenders become adults. You might think that this makes no sense as the girl is lost from the pool of prostitutes. You are wrong because the punishment creates such fear in the other girls, of which there are many, that they never cheat their Yazaks. Closing a girl, as this procedure is called, is therefore an investment. What is more, the 'closed girls' who survive become specialized at serving with their mouths and brown holes and draw a higher premium from their clients.

Running away is rare. When a child runs, recapture is almost inevitable because there is a strong honor system among the Orphanages for returning wanderers. The punishment for running is stoning. Here, the runaway is tied into a yam sack and laid on the pavement in the middle of the Orphanage. The child is then stoned; the verification of death is irrelevant, as once the fun is over, the sack is sealed and thrown into the garbage dump. The cries of pain during a stoning are so petrifying that it serves as a most effective deterrent, particularly as the punishment is delivered by those whom it seeks to deter.

Through this system of skillfully metered justice, the Orphanage is a remarkably orderly and peaceful home for children who otherwise would become street vermin.

There are no babies in the Orphanage, as they go to a separate place. Babies are highly valued, and in fact the prostitutes are discouraged from wasting their clients' issue. The babies go to a light brown tent, directly in front of the meat market, that houses upward of fifty babies and wet nurses. The babies are rented out daily to the well-organized beggar network, since a beggar with a baby gets five times more income than a childless beggar (this rule of thumb is also true for children with deformities and missing limbs). It is important to nourish the babies well enough to keep them alive but it is crucial not to overfeed them, to prevent them from becoming fat. A fat baby does not cry from hunger although a needle poked in the bottom guarantees that any living baby will cry. Babies are tattoo-marked also and have to be returned at sundown for refeeding. If a baby survives to childhood, he graduates to the Orphanage; and if not, to the dump.

How do I know all of this? My husband, Shahalad, taught me.

~

The morning after I was initiated at Master Gahil's house by the smiling uncle, Dr. Dasdaheer came to see me again. His shirt seemed to be the same crumpled one I had seen him in the day before. The doctor examined me but this time only around my vagina. He declared, as if this would lift my spirits, 'Good. No damage.' He left a folded white long-shirt on the bed for me to wear. After he left, I put it on, as I had been naked up to that point.

I lay motionless on the bed for another hour or two. Eventually the door lock clicked, the door opened, and in walked Master Gahil. The master wore a white topcoat with gold trim and he was beaming. 'Batuk, you were simply wonderful last night; congratulations, my little princess.' I stared blankly ahead of me and he continued, 'You know how much you like old Kumud's sweet-cake? That is how much your Uncle Nir loved you.' I thought of Uncle's ever-smiling face, and his shiny shoes. 'When a man becomes an uncle,' Gahil continued in his bellowing nothingness, 'he starts to like a new type of sweet-cake, and you, princess, are the most delicious of them all.' He grinned as if expecting me to laugh at his little joke. Instead I continued to stare at nothing. He inhaled deeply and continued, 'Batuk, my darling, you are special because you can help uncles feel so lovely. That makes you very, very precious, just like a princess in a palace.' He walked toward me and sat next to me on the bed. I did not look up or flinch as he carried on. 'In fact, little darling, I have made a special arrangement for you — just for you — so that you can make much, much more sweet-cake with different uncles. They will all love you so much. They will give you presents and clothes and toys and lovely, lovely food. You will see how much fun it will be; you make sweet-cakes for them and they will give you lots and lots of presents. Isn't that heaven?' I turned over and lay facedown on the bed.

He spoke to the back of my head, 'Now what do you say to your uncle Gahil?' I said nothing. The master repeated his question, 'I said, what do you say to me?' This time he did not wait for a reply. With his left hand he grasped my hair and pulled my head off the bed. With his right hand he slapped my face so hard, I thought I would black out. He slapped me again with the back of his hand (he knew not to hit me with his ringed hand). With my hair still gripped in his hand, he brought my face so close to his that I could smell his skin and feel the spit from his words land on my face. He repeated with a sneer, 'Now what do you say?' I was so shocked that I failed to even contemplate resistance. I meekly whispered, 'Thank you. Thank you, master.' He dropped my head and concluded our conversation, 'Now that's the spirit. You will have a lovely time, you lucky girl.' Then he left the room. My scalp ached and my face stung. I lay facedown on the bed once again, my cheeks sore on the soft white sheets. I remembered the old fairy tale I had read as a child and imagined that I was the princess trapped on the tiny island in the middle of a storm. The waters were rising around me and I cried out for my beloved, but even with the waters about to submerge me, he did not come.

As I lay on the bed caught in memories and dreams, I sensed I was not alone. From the back of the room, a person moved toward me. I felt rope being used to tie my wrists behind my back, and, once secured, my arms were yanked from behind me so that I rose from the bed onto my legs. I had been rewired from the girl who had entered this house just two days before into a new Batuk. Sometimes your life can change in a second and sometimes it takes a lifetime. In my case it took two days.

A hand pushed the middle of my back and propelled me through the unlocked door and out of the bedroom. I was pushed along the curtained hallway, past the dining room I had been in the previous night, along the corridor Father had delivered me to, and out through the large dark oak door. Another push half plunged me down the brick stairs onto the hot streets of Mumbai. Less than a week ago I had left my village and now I was a different vessel. I had walked up the stairs governed by my father and generations of family. Now I walked down the stairs physically restrained but aware that my existence was in my hands alone.

I was half pushed and half led to the

Orphanage by a man I never fully saw. I looked around several times and the only glimpse I got was of a broad unshaven man who looked a bit like a bulldog. I was pushed through the streets for at least an hour, and no one seemed to notice or care that a girl was being led through the streets secured with rope. Eventually, after walking through a maze of tiny streets and paths, we came to a huge clearing of bamboo ropes supporting a chessboard roof of rags: the Orphanage. I was pushed through the hordes of little children to a brick house at the far end of the expanse. As I entered the main room, the bulldog announced, 'One of Gahil's here.' His voice was deep and loud. 'Gahil says she is an easy one. He said to work her a couple of weeks, then Mamaki Briila will come and fetch her. No damage, he says.'

He left me standing at the entrance to a dark room dense with the smoke of cigarettes and hashish and lit by the glare of a television. The room was furnished with wooden couches, an assortment of scarred and repaired chairs and scattered tables, and was carpeted by a hodgepodge of worn carpets that resembled the patchwork of wafer-thin cloths that formed the roof of the Orphanage. Patches of yellow paint barely adhered to the walls. The architecture of the house was old and suggested an eternity, whereas the frenetic movements of the Yazaks reminded me of their temporary placement on earth.

'You!' a sharp, clipped voice called from the left side of the room. 'I am your husband.' Although Shahalad was physically wiry and small, his diminutive size was in contrast to his large persona. He stood with a half-stooped stance so that his head was cocked back at all times, which not only shortened him but gave him the appearance of always sniffing at the air. His bent-back head coupled with his quick and shifting gaze made him look like a rat. Shahalad was not the highest-ranking Yazak but was not the lowest-ranking either. He had a status among his peers that gave me a status among mine. When he announced me as his bride, there were roars of mockery, to which he responded with a large, even white grin.

If I had hoped that my nuptials would be protracted, I was to be disappointed. As soon as the roars of mockery died down, Shahalad said in a strong voice that had a slow, even rhythm and sounded completely alien to his small physique that it was time to take his new wife to her wedding feast. He grasped my wrist and led me toward the back of the room amid calls of 'Does she know what gifts you have for her?' 'Don't honeymoon too long,' and, in a mocking high-pitched tone, 'Darling, darling, I love you.'

~

In the Orphanage everything was done in haste. Shahalad led me to a back room in the building that was lit only from the main room. He pushed me up against a wall and lifted my white smock, and I felt him try to push his bhunnas into me from behind, with one hand on the back of my neck. He was fumbling and panting. He cursed. He soon realized that he could not maneuver me to couple with him in the way he envisioned. He threw me down onto a mattress on the floor covered with a threadbare blanket. He split my legs apart, lay on top of me, and pushed himself into me. He had far more strength than I had imagined, although I did not fight hard against him — perhaps this was a result of my rewiring. He had not said a word since we entered the room. He completed a handful of thrusts before I felt his terminal pulsations. As he finished, he rolled off me onto his back. I could sense that words were percolating inside him but he did not speak. We both lay on our backs, silently looking at the dark featureless ceiling of this cell.

At that moment, the darkness was punctuated by the shouts of the Yazaks and the television noise from the main room. I could feel my identity separating from my body. When you create a painting, you apply paint to canvas; it is a mechanical process whereby a brush is dipped in paint and smeared over the canvas. As a masterpiece is painted, however, there comes a moment when the picture is no longer only a mere representation but possesses the essence of the artist. At this moment an unquantifiable element has been added to the canvas; you cannot weigh it and you cannot see it, but there it is! It is soul.

In that dark little cell, I willed my soul free of my body. My soul jumped onto the spinning upper air that covers the top of the earth and there she was unconfined. I roared across the upper air and kissed Navaj goodnight, moved Mother's favorite necklace so that she could not find it in the morning, and watched Father because he needs me to. I swirled at the feet of the great poets and rode in the manes of the swiftest horses. I filled the silent caves of the mountains and I confused the eagle as he was about to snap his talons over a field mouse (and so contravened 'will'). I ignored the dying, for they will soon join me here, but helped the sick taste their pain. I laughed at the same blindness that the poor and rich share. All this, as I lay next to my silent husband.

The stillness that hung in our space was splintered by Shahalad suddenly jumping to his feet; I had thought he was asleep. As he shot from the cell, he stopped short, spun round, and came back to where I lay. He stood over me and looked down. There was a jingle in his eyes and a smile on his face that were not altogether unattractive. He then turned away and left me.

As Shahalad entered the main room, I could hear cheers from the Yazaks. 'What a man' was one. After a short while my husband returned to the cell. I half expected another round of sweet-cake but no, he bade me enter the main room with him. I did as I was asked. Once I had gotten onto my feet, my body was not in pain, but I felt his juice sliding down my thigh. As I entered the main room behind Shahalad, I was barraged with the verbiage of the mindless: 'You lucky bitch, to get a man with such a small penis,' and 'Are you ready girl for the main course?' I stared intently at the floor and noticed the smoothness of the bricks worn down by centuries of feet.

It was clear that my beauty served

Shahalad well, as he frequently glanced at me from different points of the room as he mingled there. I saw children come and go from the main room; on each occasion they sought out their respective Yazak to presumably gain orders and collect rewards. I soon learned that everyone was taken at their word at the Orphanage. The Yazaks never verified that a task was complete and issued rewards as verbal requisitions: 'Tell cook So-and-so to give you rice and meat' (a rare treat). Since disobedience was so brutally enforced, contravening a Yazak's order carried enormous risk and necessitated stupidity. Some of the brutality was not judicial but unchecked sadism. For example, I saw a child (maybe eight) executed for threatening another child with a knife. The Yazak made the guilty child kneel and then he knelt behind him, holding the boy tightly in his arms. The Yazak made the other child slit the restrained boy's throat while the now-silent crowd watched. Rape was common too; an older prostitute or even a girl would be brought into the main room, tied to a table facedown, and left there stripped to pleasure any man who wanted her. I knew not to interfere and learned that obedience was unquestioned and that the value of life is a moment; that was the unspoken creed of the Yazak.

On my second day, Wolf, who was the head of the Yazaks, called across the room, 'Shah, I am going to take your wife for a cup of tea to make sure she is settling in well and you are treating her right.' Wolf was not like the other Yazaks. The others, Shahalad included, were dirty and wore rags, whereas Wolf dressed tidily. Today, for example, he wore a spotless white shirt, pressed denim jeans, and brown leather shoes. Similarly, he was well groomed. He was clean shaven, wore his hair neatly combed, and had well-defined facial features. He was neither ugly nor handsome. His most remarkable physical feature was that he looked like a fourteen-year-old child when in fact he was far older. He gave an impression of innocence.

The Yazaks feared Wolf. They never spoke of him when he was not there for fear of another Yazak ratting on them. When he came into the main room, there was an utter hush, and when Wolf issued an order there was absolute obedience. I never once saw his authority questioned. Another interesting thing about Wolf was that he did not live in the Orphanage, like the Yazaks, but somewhere in the city. He would show up in the main room at odd times to speak with the most senior Yazaks or sometimes just to watch television, but then he would leave.

At least once a week, he would bring his light tan briefcase, which contained neatly apportioned sachets of white and brown powders, multicolored tablets, and brown-looking pieces of wood. Orphans, who had been organized by the Yazaks, were used to deliver the sachets throughout the city. On all the occasions I saw Wolf, he never raised his voice and always smiled. The orphans loved to see him as he always had sweets, a coin, or a kind word for them. His outward appearance of kind innocence was effective and remarkably deceptive.

Wolf beckoned me to him and I obeyed; there was a tangible power to him. 'What is your name, little one?' he asked. 'Batuk,' I answered, eyes downcast. 'Batuk. That's a nice name. I just want to have a cup of tea with you and make sure that scallywag Shahalad is being good to you. Master Gahil specifically asked that you have a nice time here as he has good plans for you. Let's go somewhere a bit more private.' As Wolf led me toward the back rooms, the sea of Yazaks, orphans, and whores split apart before us. When we got to one of the larger rooms, one of the Yazaks, who had followed us, laid out a clean-looking blanket over the mattress and then left us. Wolf spoke so softly that I could just hear him over the noise from the main room: 'Batuk, kneel down.' I knelt before him and he continued to speak softly to me. 'I am called Wolf, and my job is to take care of everyone ... ' With that he removed his bhunnas from his trousers and pushed my face onto it. It was soft and doughy. I knew what I was supposed to do. He continued as I moistened and licked him, 'I have to make sure, you see, that everyone ... you, Shahalad, Gahil ... is organized and happy. Master Gahil, for example, needs to make sure that you will work well for him so that he can take care of you.' He was responding to the warmth and wetness of my mouth. He carried on, 'You will need to work hard for Gahil if you want nice clothes and toys ... ' He pulled my face off him. His bhunnas was sticking straight out from his body. I watched from my knees as he took a little sachet from his pocket and sprinkled white powder along its length. 'Batuk,' he continued, 'here is a little treat for you. Lick the sugar off ... be a good girl.' The sugar did not taste sweet at all but had a bitter taste. As he guided my head over the stretched, bitter skin, a glaring, screaming bright light came on in my head ... I was going to explode but I gave myself to Wolf.

I woke up at night on the mattress. The blanket had been removed. I was in pain and completely naked. Most of all my neck hurt. My hair was wet and cold and the room smelled bad. I looked around. Shahalad was sitting at the far end of the cell watching me. When he saw me wake up, he folded his lips into his mouth like he was sucking on a lollipop. As much pain as I felt, I could see that he too grieved — maybe for me or maybe for him.

Shahalad got up, walked over to me, and stood over me. I could not read his eyes, as it was dark. He slipped off his trousers (he did not wear shoes) and climbed onto me. He jammed into me with so much anger that I thought he would crush my body, but he did not. As he was releasing himself, I recognized the smell on my hair as urine.

~

Shahalad was not a demanding husband, as I was predominantly a showpiece for him. This was a role I was happy to play. The more I attested to his potency, the less potent he seemed to need to be. In fact, within a week, he would drag me into the back room (I had learned to scream in mock fear) and there we would sit, sometimes for hours. While we sat together on the mattress, I would scream out in feigned agony from time to time or beg for 'more.' This was entirely my idea and it pleased him.

Our times together in the cell varied. Sometimes Shahalad would fall on me and make sweet-cake but this was always short-lived and became less painful as I became habituated. Also with habituation I gained greater skill at releasing myself to the upper air. There were other times when he would speak to me. He would most often speak of events at the Orphanage. He told me of the beatings and the cruelties, I think to dissipate his own pain. He would tell me about Wolf's exploits in part out of admiration and in part out of hatred. Once he mentioned a dead brother, but he never said anything else about himself or his family. Once he told me that he liked me. He did not seem to expect me to say anything, which was just as well, as I had nothing to say. There were other occasions when we would sit together in perfect silence. He would smoke and we shared serenity together. There were occasions when I wished that those times would never end and I think he wished this too.

Between sessions with Shahalad in the back room, there was little else for me to do, and so most of the time I would sit doing nothing in the main room. I favored a wooden bench at the back of the room where I could sit or lie down and just watch the goings-on. I was happy to be alone most of the time. The other girls, by contrast, would parade themselves around the main room. Just as there was a hierarchy among the Yazaks, there was a similar pecking order among the wives. They would expose their thighs or uncovered breasts. They would flirt with Yazaks who were not their husbands, which often resulted in terrific fights among jealous wives. Sometimes wives would contribute to the punishment of a street prostitute who was brought to the main room for 'correctional teaching' for becoming lazy or unproductive; here a wife might help tie down a woman or even goad a Yazak to 'split her.' I once saw a wife push a beer bottle into one particularly ugly street girl, saying, 'That should get her going.' I observed a savagery among the wives, some barely older than me, the motivation for which I suspect was simply survival. I happily melted into my chair at the back of the room and sought invisibility.

For most of the time the Yazaks, other than Shahalad, left me alone. There was a strict code that one Yazak did not take another's wife to the cells and I never saw this rule violated. Wolf of course was the exception. I was not Wolf's favorite and he never took me to the cells again, although every time I caught a glimpse of him or felt his eyes glancing on me, I smarted and felt the hairs on my body stiffen. My bruises from him soon healed. Another Yazak's wife was Wolf's chosen one, a very tall, stunningly beautiful older woman who reveled in Wolf's attention and oftentimes mocked her husband publicly, knowing that she was untouchable; that was until one day she just disappeared. I soon realized that Wolf welcomed all the new wives personally and loved to evoke fear and hatred in each. His dominance over the wives implied the same over the husbands. A couple of years later, when I was on the Common Street, I heard that the Yazaks eventually turned on Wolf and hacked him to pieces with knives and broken bottles. His evisceration was so complete that he was taken to the dump in two dozen brown paper bags. It is the nature of great leaders to rise and fall.

~

It was during my second week at the Orphanage that I first met Puneet. In the midday heat, I had been taken to the back

137

room by Shahalad where he briefly made sweet-cake with me before we both fell asleep. We were awakened by a commotion in the main room and Shahalad jumped up and ran out. A few minutes later, I lolled into the main room and headed for my seat at the back of the room. There, in my chair, sat Puneet; he was eight at the time, a beautiful-looking boy. He sat with his knees drawn to his chin, dried tears on his face. His black hair was dusty and he was thin. He had been sucked off the street.

Like many hungry street boys, Puneet had been caught pilfering food from the market and had been sent to the Orphanage. This is the way many children arrive there; they are caught committing small crimes, say by a vendor, by another member of the Orphanage, or even by the police. A Yazak is then called to cart them away and bring them to the Orphanage. When the Yazak came to collect Puneet from the fruit seller who had caught him, he was tied to a lamppost by his neck and hands. The Yazak immediately saw Puneet's potential as a love-boy. These boys either become prized as being male or become girl-boys — boys who get dressed as girls. Puneet inevitably became a girl-boy because of his femininity. He had been deposited by the Yazak at the brick hut while

Shahalad and I had been sleeping. Wolf had immediately taken him, before assigning him to a Yazak, and broken him; new girl-boys were Wolf's greatest pleasure. I had actually heard Puneet's shrieks a few hours before but I had thought nothing of them, as these sorts of noises formed part of the air in the Orphanage. Wolf had been at him for hours before an emergency at the Orphanage had occurred, which had necessitated his cutting the boy free.

As Wolf became immersed in the mounting crisis, I sat next to Puneet and we watched in silence as the Yazaks congregated in the middle of the room with Wolf at their center. The issue of concern was that another Orphanage had started to traffic stolen goods through our territory. The demarcation between the three major Orphanages was well defined and rarely infringed upon. Clearly today was the exception. Wolf, who always spoke softly, urged caution. For the only time I ever observed it, one of the senior Yazaks disagreed with him, asserting that they needed to defend their territory aggressively. I could not see exactly what happened because of the crowd, but this Yazak ran from the middle of the huddle screaming, with blood pouring from his cheek. Everyone else seemed to agree with Wolf's approach.

The crisis of the trafficking violations absorbed the Yazaks' attention for the entire night. This resulted in my sharing several uninterrupted hours alone with Puneet. I remained sitting next to him for the whole time, watching the goings-on, but he did not apparently notice or care. Since I was accustomed to sitting alone in silence for hours, Puneet's silence was no inconvenience to me at all. We sat together, alone, in silence.

Generally, when night came, the Yazaks took their wives to the back rooms. Many couples shared rooms as there were more Yazaks than there were rooms. (Some couples also slept in the main room.) Tonight was different, as the Yazaks who had not left with Wolf to investigate what had happened stayed behind but were hushed and tense. A cricket game was on the television but the room was otherwise silent. Eventually I saw Puneet's eyelids start to droop and soon his head flopped to the side and he fell asleep. I slid off the bench to let him lie down. As he fell sideways, I saw a puddle of blood on the seat where his bottom had been; the blood was already dry and darkening. I slept on the floor at his feet.

Wolf proved to be correct. What had occurred, I learned later, was that a single rogue gang of house thieves had strayed into our territory. The matter was quickly resolved that night when Wolf and several of our Yazaks met with the equivalent leadership from the other Orphanage. Apparently reparations were made; Shahalad did not know exactly what they were but we both guessed that the rogue gang had become part of the great garbage mound of Mumbai.

The following night I dreamed for the first time of the hat vendor at the market. Though I did not yet know I would see this dream several times in the future, even then it puzzled me. It was such a realistic experience that I awoke with a start in the middle of the night, trying to grab the falling hats. I felt that my descent through the marketplace was a premonition. Truth proved me to be right because three days later I was collected by Mamaki Briila.

When Mamaki Briila entered the main room, the Yazaks called her 'Hippopotamus' to her face. She did not seem to take offense but rather laughed at the endearment. Hippopotamus and I left for the Common Street on foot — I was unbound. I had no idea that Puneet's destiny was married to mine but a few weeks later he showed up to occupy the nest two doors down from mine. I never got to say goodbye to Shahalad.

He may have laughed yesterday at the joke about the disappearance of Hippopotamus's husband, but Puneet is a sullen pile of horseshit. He is no use to me as he sits downcast all the time. Pah!

Looking down the street, I can see an old man. He is gray and stooped and he is walking up the Common Street toward me. He is wearing an oversized brown suit and in his right hand he is holding a shiny steel walking stick. The base of the stick has three prongs, each with its own black rubber cap. The stick seems to be indestructible but everything else about him is brittle. It seems that his grasp on life is as tenuous as a word caught beneath an eraser.

Each time he advances his walking stick, he resembles a watchmaker meticulously placing a cog in a watch mechanism. Once the stick has been placed about a handbreadth in front of the old man, the left leg advances six inches: *sh,sh,sh*. Once the left leg has reached its target, a pause occurs. Then the right leg follows: *sh,sh,sh*. He could be excused this slowness were he to possess everlasting life, in which case time would be inconsequential. However, it is obvious that he is shuffling along the edge of the well of death. Perhaps he is afraid that if he slips, he will fall into the well.

What is funniest of all, however, is that as he walks in this excruciating unhurried manner, he is grasping his testicles in his left hand, as if they are about to fall off. His grasp on them is so tight that I can see the whites of his knuckles. I peer at him, but he looks ahead, completely expressionless. I swear I have watched him for an hour and he has walked fifty paces. I guarantee he will not bake sweet-cake with me. Mind you, if he did, I would need to set the day aside. I was going to point him out to Puneet, but why bother?

Oh calamity! Coming from the other end of the Common Street, down the hill, is Mr. Bent-Nose for his weekly cooking session. You should have seen him the first time he baked with me. Sweat formed a river down his back and his 'thank you' resembled the stutter of the old man's gait. But here Bent-Nose comes, gaily bouncing down the street as if on his way to a birthday party.

~

As Mr. Bent-Nose reassembled himself and prepared to depart from my nest, he pecked me on the cheek as if bidding a favored niece farewell. He said, 'I have done you a favor, my sweetest.' To be honest, he had already done me a favor by finishing his sweet-cake in five minutes yet staying with me for an hour. He continued, 'A senior manager from my company' (I had no idea what he did, except that I was sure he did it badly) 'was asking around the office if anyone knew a pretty girl for a party. I told him to come down here and get the girl with the green curtain over her . . . room.' 'Oooh,' I said (I had no idea of his name and I certainly could not call him Mr. Bent-Nose), 'you are so kind to me. I will have something extra special for you next time.' I drew him to me and embraced him. After I had expressed my extreme gratitude, which I knew would delight him, I forgot him.

Late that night, after the night rush, a taxi drove down the Common Street and stopped close to our nests. A man got out of the white car. In silhouette he appeared to be quite handsome. He was large and full figured and effused power like fresh tea. From the taxi headlamps I saw that he wore a light blue suit. It is astonishing how quickly Mamaki can move when the nectar of money is puffed in her nostrils; she sprung on the man with the agility of a mountain goat. The man stared in the direction of my nest. My green curtain was partly drawn and the small electric light lit me from the back. I am not sure if he saw my face, but he stared at me for longer than a glance. I then remembered the earlier comment of Mr. Bent-Nose. The man spoke with Mamaki for several minutes and looked over at me again. He climbed back into the taxi, which sped off, just missing an elderly woman carrying heavy sacks to the Street of Thieves before the protection of darkness lifted. Even after the taxi had disappeared, Hippopotamus was still waving goodbye, a huge smile on her face.

The next day, something out of the ordinary was in the air; I could taste it. My supper tray contained rice, meat, fruit, and lassi, and as I started to eat, Mamaki waddled into my nest and sat beside me on my throne. She was flushed with excitement and overexertion, desperate to talk. She spoke like the mad people who have more words to get out than their lips can speak: 'Batuk, darling, the man who came last night . . . ' (puff, puff) 'the one in the taxi . . . ' (puff, puff) ' . . . he is going to send a car for you later and take you to a hotel . . . for a treat. A hotel!' She repeated 'hotel' as if it were heaven. 'Now, darling,' she said, as an insincere smile slid onto her face, 'you spend as long as you like there and you do a good job for me . . . I

145

promise you, Batuk, you will be eating like this for weeks.' She was spitting all over me as she spoke; it was disgusting. However, I could see that this was something to celebrate and so I smiled.

Now I am alone again. I have not felt fear since the night I met my new uncles but now that feeling has returned.

This ends the blue notebook.

*Numbered sheets of paper from
the Royal Imperial Hotel, Mumbai*

About an hour after nightfall, a white taxi drew up outside my nest. Mamaki was obviously waiting in the shadows as she sprang out like a disturbed bullfrog. She was smiling and bowing; it was quite comical. At one point, I thought her breast might fall out of her dress but thankfully the steel struts of her brassiere held fast. After she had bowed at least a dozen times, the same man as earlier, still wearing the light blue suit, got out of the taxi. He handed Mamaki an envelope, which she took and opened. She turned her back to him, pulled out the deepest pile of money I had ever seen, and counted it while mumbling to herself. Halfway through the pile, she looked over to me. 'Batuk, Batuk, go on, get in the car. Off you go.' The taxi driver, a tall, fat man who wore a sand-colored army uniform, got out of the car. The uniform was dirty and he smelled as unclean as any of my cooks. He said to me in a tone of disdain dressed in false politeness, 'Get in the car

. . . next to me.' The politeness, I figured, was for the sake of the man in the light blue suit.

'Batuk, is it?' said the man in the light blue suit from the rear of the car. The car had pulled off. I had made sweet-cake in the front seat and backseat of cars and so I was familiar with driving through the streets like this. I love the music that comes from the radio. I am not fussy about what sort of music I listen to, but I find it irresistible how sound moves through itself and how it rises and falls. I have no idea how music can evoke feelings, but I can dissolve my own rhythm inside its beat.

I was itching to ask for music in the car but did not dare to. The driver turned his head to me as we turned off the Common Street and spoke to me with unfettered loathing. 'The gentleman spoke to you . . . did you not hear?' I realized I was developing a severe headache, the feeling of a wet strip of material tightening around my forehead. I felt a wave of despair and I wanted to vomit. 'Batuk,' I replied to my knees. 'Speak up,' the driver ordered. 'I heard just fine' came the voice from behind my right shoulder. The man in the light blue suit talked like silk. 'So it's Batuk. That's an unusual name,' he said. 'Look, Batuk, there is no need to be afraid; I just want you to meet a friend of mine. If it does not work out, no harm done. Is that all right?' With each word, the band around my head tightened just a little. I turned my head toward the man in the backseat. The blue of his suit hurt my eyes. I drove a smile through my head and onto my face with the force of an ax that breaks stone. I said, 'Thank you, sir, that is fine.' He responded in kind. 'Batuk, you are so pretty, I am sure my friend will love you.'

I faced forward and watched the Mumbai night stream by. As we stopped at a traffic light, three beggar boys accosted the car; one had a massive lump projecting from his neck, the other a glazed left eye, and the third a severed arm. It is well known that deformed boys are the most valuable as beggars and it was quite possible that a Yazak from one of the Orphanages had chopped off the third boy's arm to increase his value. Regardless of the boys' appeal, our windows remained closed and we continued on. As we drove alongside the promenade, I saw the ocean for the first time. Palm trees dotted the boardwalk, lit up by strings of electric lights. Food vendors sold hot food from rusted grills and fruit from makeshift stands. Well-dressed foreigners and Indians ambled along, some with children. These people appeared different from the people I saw parading along the Common Street every day. They were clean and orderly and did not leer; they often smiled and laughed. On the other hand, these well-dressed rich were also merely a stream of human life that flowed this way and that. Watching them going places I could not see, I felt that I presided over this river of humanity. Perhaps the tree had spoken the truth, that it was all created for me.

Every now and again, groups of beggars emerged from the shadows to accost the wealthy walkers but retreated in response to a dismissive sweep of the hand. I saw one Indian spit at one of the beggars. We drove too fast for me to see the beggar's response.

~

The hotel was a huge sand-colored stone building with massive windows. Through the windows, I could see enormous chandeliers hanging from an invisible ceiling. There was a lit veranda immediately over the entranceway, where hotel guests could look out over the waterfront while drinking cocktails, safe from the advances of beggars. Mamaki had been right; this was magnificent. I was not in rags but wore the glaring bright red chiffon of my trade. I caught my reflection in the window as I entered the hotel behind the gentleman in the light blue suit. I was not clean but my physical beauty burst through the dirt of the streets as fire through rice paper.

I stepped into a massive, spinning glass door. A fifteen-year-old girl, with the evolving body of womanhood, stepped out of the magical glass entry into her palace. I had tight hips, fist-sized breasts, and the poise of royalty. Hidden in my vest, my nipples had grown and were deepening in color. My armpits and my vagina had grown the early hair that retains the scent that draws men astray and causes them to behave outside themselves. I halted my step as we walked across the entranceway and looked momentarily at my reflection in the windows. People peered up from their papers and men looked away from their wives. It may have been because I wore no shoes and they did.

I followed the blue-suited man through the palace entrance hall. The unknowing eyes watching us wondered, a father and daughter? An uncle and niece? The reality was an emissary and prostitute. We entered a box that contained a man dressed to serve, who was ordered to the seventeenth floor by the emissary. The doors of the box closed. I would have felt afraid were it not for the man in the light blue suit standing next to me. I looked around for a hole in the floor as I thought it might be a toilet. It was too small for a throne room. Then the box jolted. Heat rushed to my neck. Then it moved and I held my breath. But the box then sang to me, a strange soft growling sound. 'Batuk,' it said, 'welcome to my temple.' As the doors to the box slid open, I let out my breath. We were in a new place, the gates to a temple; and before me sat the gatekeeper.

An old man in a white cotton shirt and pants sat on a simple wooden chair outside a pair of giant open doors. He wore a straw hat and no shoes and stared downward at the floor. We walked past the man as if we were invisible into a room the proportions of which I had never imagined. My headache had completely disappeared. I was overwhelmed by space.

I realized that the size of the room appeared even greater than it was because the ceiling was so high. Everything shone. To my left, through an entryway, was another room, in which I could see a huge bed covered in lime green. Along the right side of the room was a polished wooden table with six chairs around it. In front of me was an arrangement of two large sofas and two single armchairs. A television as tall as myself was housed in its own wooden cabinet facing the sofas. The seating encircled a glass table, on which lay a fan of books. Even the books were big, their covers shiny, reflecting the light of a chandelier overhead.

For all its grandeur, the room was dominated by the wall decoration directly facing me. Splayed across the wall were the skin and head of a tiger. The head faced downward, as if the tiger were trying to crawl off the wall. He and I locked eyes; he seemed to be smiling, perhaps because he was happy to have been killed and hung up for his eternal rest in a palace as lavish as this. Below the tiger's head, two crossed silver swords hung on the wall, to suggest that the tiger had been killed with these weapons. I doubted the tiger was slain in a just sword-fight; man rarely relinquishes power for the sake of fairness.

Impulsively, I started to walk around the room. The softness of the carpet made me feel as if I walked on clouds. The man in the light blue suit was looking in his wallet for something and did not seem to be in a hurry. I went from chair to chair touching their soft backs, over to the dining table and then to the entrance of the bedroom. Although I was flooded with things to see and smell (the space smelled so clean), I did not lose sight of why I had been brought here. I turned to face the man in the light blue suit, who had remained standing by the door and who was now looking at me while turning a small white card in his hand.

As I looked over to him, he called out 'Hita' in the direction of the bedroom. I half expected to see the nurse from the hospital appear with her huge, lovely chubby smile. An amazing thought flitted through my mind that Hita had married well (obviously not the teacher) and had come to rescue me and have me as her daughter (this would have been fine with me). Such fantasies have the lifespan of a raindrop; by the time you see it, it has landed, exploded, and disappeared. The Hita that emerged from the bedroom was trim and had none of the transparent happiness of her namesake. She marched through the bedroom door as if she had been called for an important business meeting. She looked straight ahead of her, her face like her body, lean and purposeful. 'Yes, Mr. Vas?' she asked in a clipped but polite tone. She wore a plain white cotton suit with red-and-white lining. Everything about her outward appearance was plain and functional, but I could sense other depths to her that she hid. The man in the light blue suit said, 'Here is Batuk.' He turned to me and said, 'Hita will clean you up and look after you; anything you need, just ask her. I will see you tomorrow.' He smiled without warmth and left.

~

The door closed behind the disappearing suit of blue; it appeared that the elderly doorman had fallen asleep, for he jumped as the emissary left. Hita turned toward me and looked me up and down like a dress. She folded her arms and said to me, 'Little whore, don't you ever forget that I know exactly what you are. Don't you dare play princess with me or you will see my hand.' I did not say a word but I knew that she would never lay a hand on me, as I was obviously here to please a master of hers, perhaps the man in blue or perhaps someone else. Even if she did strike me, her threat was toothless since, from the looks of her, she could not possibly inflict sufficient pain on me that I would care; you see, I am quite inoculated to pain. However, I recognized that buying favor from Hita might be convenient and so I feigned subservience.

Puneet would have loved to have seen my performance. Actress Batuk fell to the floor in front of Hita, knelt, and placed my forehead on the carpet's softness. I implored her, 'Oh mistress, I beg of you. Please, please do not strike me. I have been hit so often, mistress. Whatever you order me to do, I will. I promise.' Yes! I even managed to command tears to my face so that when I looked up at her from my prostrate position at her feet, my eyes were swollen. She was obviously moved by my performance; she actually leaned down to me and offered me her hand. 'Batuk, come, stand up; there's no need to cry. I really won't hurt you; you have my word. Come on, sweetheart, get up.' I took her hand, pulled myself up, and felt guilty for my well-acted deceit.

I then started to cry. The first tear rolled down my left cheek. The second tear followed the first. Then I felt a tear from my right eye, this one not born of duplicity but of pure, torrid, and unfettered despair. The first tear had slid down my cheek, hung upon my chin, and fell to the carpet; the other two tears followed the first. And then I was sobbing. I had not cried since the day I had been left with Master Gahil many years before. All my feelings of being alone in a world awhirl with evil erupted and all the feelings of being cut off from the strands of my true life compounded. Suddenly, the lakes of love that had become buried deep within me started to pour out of me. Hita held me to her thin chest and I closed my eyes to enter the darkness.

She lowered her chin to my head, stroked my hair slowly, and said nothing. And then I knew that it was not Hita's touch and it was not her person and it was not the beautiful room and it was not the hundreds of men and it was not the black ink; it was the smell of the river on Hita's clothes that had released the flood of tears. As I inhaled her I smelled the river, the same river that as a child I had bathed in, washed clothes in, swum in, and drunk from. On her, I smelled the same source as my own. But then, as my spirit opened into this woman, I understood that it was she who smelled of the river and not her clothes, it was she who was the river. As I cried, rivulets of tears dripped into the channel that formed naturally between her meager breasts. I melted into that river and she with me. We were neither as two lovers nor as a child suckling, but we were as one because we were one water together. If you mix water from one cup with water from another, can you distinguish them? No! They are the same water; there is no separation. The bodies of women, so gently carved, are the skins that carry water over the earth. Like one glass of water poured into another, I poured into Hita and she mixed into me so that we became a single drop.

Men are seekers. Men seek to stream into

us from their wet mouths, their sweat, and their sex. All that they seek, however, is to return into the river that is woman. Why is that? Man emanates from the water of woman; he is carried there, until at birth he swims from it. Then, what is the first thing man does when he leaves us? He seeks to suck and draw the river into him, for without woman, he is empty. For the rest of his life man deposits his sins and waste back into the river. In the end, his dead body burns before returning to the river that is woman.

What is hardship — that I am the vehicle of his want? His sex emptying into me or dribbling down the edges of my mouth — is that truly hardship or is that my role as his vessel? If a seeker is all that man is, then I am a bowl. It is nature for him to seek his source. Here I stand, thrown from earth's clay, pigmented for his delight, and then hardened through extreme heat. Here I am, his bowl. He may smash me but it is folly to do so, for it is I whom he seeks. It is his nature to want to empty into me and mine to receive him. The hardship of woman knows this. But be cautious. Some of us have holes, others are cracked, and still others are so delicate that one knock can destroy us. Some of us are not glazed and, to be frank, some of us appear ugly but have a remarkable capacity. It does not matter, for as bowls, we receive them and in us they reside. Swishing around, we carefully approach the river and pour them back from where they came.

I am a lake of unimaginable depth and inestimable volume that is a confluence of all men.

As Hita and I separated she said, 'Batuk, let me run you a bath.'

The bathroom was as magnificent as the other rooms in the Tiger Suite. It was walled with light brown polished stone. There were two polished sinks with silver taps, white towels, a toilet, and a bathtub. The toilet was made from white stone and shone like the sink. It had its own cover that lifted upward. To the left of the toilet, built into the wall, was a paper roll with a tongue of paper hanging down ready to lick your bottom. The bath was big enough to fit an ox. Three stone steps led up to the bath, the same stone used for the walls. The water in the tub was steaming and the layer of soap bubbles that floated on its surface was so thick that it looked as though you needed a knife to cut it.

I walked up the steps as if I were ascending the Queen's throne and stepped into the bath like a drunkard cutting his top lip into a glass of beer. As I sunk into the heat, I remembered the last time I had been immersed in a bath full of hot water; on the last occasion it was the old woman who had scrubbed me and on this occasion it was to be Hita.

First, Hita cleaned my hair. Her fingers massaged the shampoo into my scalp and she rubbed my long, thick hair between her palms to clean it. She applied the shampoo three times, each time showering off the soap with warm water. Soap streamed down my neck into the bubbles; water returning to water. She wrapped my hair in a towel and I lay back in the bath and she washed my body. The pressure of her fingertips was intense and almost painful as she moved her hands back and forth over my back, shoulders, and neck. My body arched in response. But when she cleaned my arms and my breasts she raised her fingertips off my skin and sunk the palms of her hands downward, giving an altogether different sensation. When she washed my breasts my nipples became firm. Although my breasts were only the size of oranges, there was fullness to them. Her hands lingered there and her back-and-forth hand motion slowed. With each hand action she accentuated the friction of her palms on my now-erect dark nipples, and without prompting, my legs flexed imperceptibly under the hot water.

She next started to clean my legs. Both of her hands encircled my left ankle and moved along my calf in long, firm strokes. She pressed hard into the muscles and I felt tension that I did not know existed release. Her sunken hazel eyes followed her hands as she repeated these movements on my right calf, but from there she started to strongly massage my thigh. As her hands cleaned my inner thigh, a belt tightened around my belly and a soft sound slipped from my lips. Her hands moved across to my left thigh. My eyes shut and her hands rhythmically washed up and down the whole leg but this time with each long caress, the edge of her hand nudged against my bunny rabbit's ears. Reflexively I let my legs part a little. Feelings from my belly showered downward. She pulled her hands from the water and lathered soap onto her right hand, which she then placed flat against my swollen ears and rubbed firmly back and forth to clean it. I opened my eyes for an instant and I saw that she was now staring at me. 'Batuk,' she whispered, 'let's get you out.'

I stepped from the bath into a large white towel that Hita held for me, being careful not to let the towel on my head fall off. 'Darling, go and lie on the bed,' she said, 'and I will be there in a second.' I went and lay facedown on top of the pale green bedspread, my head turned to the bathroom entrance, watching Hita. She came from the bathroom carrying a tray, with her sleeves rolled up and a soft, self-assured smile on her face. She placed the tray next to me on the bed and said sweetly, 'Batuk, I want you to relax . . . would you like me to put on some music?' I nodded. She knelt down and switched on the radio built into the bed's headboard, tuning it to a station playing sitar music. 'Lie on your back,' she instructed. As I rolled onto my back Hita undid the towel with a gentle confidence and it fell open. I lay naked except for my hair. She said, 'Just relax and put your arms over your head.' With a big brown brush she wiped cream under my armpit nearest her and using a razor shaved off the early grasses of womanhood. She repeated this on the other arm and then wiped my shaved armpits with a towel that had been moistened with warm water. She told me to relax my arms and I let them fall by my sides. She took the brush from the tray, dipped it in cream, and wiped it over my entire rabbit face. The ears were

162

quite swollen from the rubbing and the heat of the bath and the cream felt tingly. 'Just relax,' Hita said as she shaved, down to up. She started at my inner thigh and swept upward with short strokes. I squiggled a bit with the feeling. Once she was finished, she used another warm, moist towel to clean me. My dew was leaking from me and I could smell myself.

'There, finished,' Hita said. 'Come slip under the covers.' I obligingly did so and she smiled at me. 'You have a long day tomorrow and you need your rest. Sleep well.' I looked up at her to return her smile but then had to look again, for all I saw was emptiness. That night, I had no dreams.

~

I was awakened by shafts of light sliding through the cracks between the curtains and shining into my eyes. I was alone in the room. I climbed out of bed and started to explore.

The Tiger Suite comprised the three rooms I already knew: the bedroom, the bathroom, and the living area. I went into the living room, where Tiger smiled at me and bade me good morning. 'Yes, I did sleep well. Did you?' I answered his inquiry. I dragged the window curtain and found that it glided open weightlessly. I saw the turquoise of the ocean illuminated by blazing sunshine. The water extended to eternity. The sunshine was early in its day's travel and shone straight at me. Far, far below was the wide promenade on which only a few people walked. I saw a couple of people in brightly colored outfits running from an invisible demon. Between the promenade and the hotel was the street; cars and buses drove unimpeded. I opened all the curtains one by one, first in the living room and then in the bedroom. Three of the tall windows (two in the living room and one in the bedroom) faced the water and I felt that if I stepped from the window, I would walk straight into the ocean. The bedroom had a second window that was set at right angles to the ocean front. This one looked down onto a side street where I saw five tiny men repairing a dirty dark green car. Then it struck me that I was naked.

It was not that I felt ashamed about being unclothed, but I had not been naked in private for as long as I could remember. Of course, I was naked for the weekly shower with the other girls and Puneet, which we had in the wet room behind Hippo's lair, but apart from that I was always clothed. In my nest, which seemed a lifetime away, I could have slept naked with my curtain drawn if I had wanted to but it never crossed my mind to do so. Although the tiger and I were both naked and we loved the feeling of the sun's glare on our bodies, I felt it immodest to be undressed.

In the bathroom I found a heavy white robe made from thick toweling. It was obviously sized for a man, but once the sleeves were rolled up, it served me perfectly. I tied the sash round my waist and headed to the entrance of the Tiger Suite. I said to the tiger, 'Don't worry, I am not leaving. I am just going to pop out for a bit to explore.' He growled his approval and I smiled. The door was locked from the outside, however. I put my ear to it and could swear that I heard the old doorman breathing. Popping out was obviously not an option.

I noticed a bowl of fruit on the dining table. I was tremendously hungry and assumed that it was for me. I took a large, soft mango from the bowl, peeled half of it with my teeth and fingers, and buried my face in the sweet pulp. My face was covered in mango juice when I heard a key jangling in the door. Hita strode in before I could wipe all the mango off. I looked guiltily across the room at her. She smiled in amusement. 'I see you are hungry,' she said.

'Let's order breakfast for you. What do you like to eat?' I milled the question through my mind. I had no real idea what I liked. I eventually answered, 'Anything is fine . . . thank you, Miss Hita.'

Hita spoke on the phone for a short while. She switched on the television to a program where a woman was talking about an apartment building that had caught fire. They were showing pictures of charred bodies and it reminded me of the dump behind the Orphanage. I had preferred the silence and solitude that preceded Hita's arrival but such matters were not my choice. I thought fleetingly of my husband.

After a while, there was a knock at the door and a man in a white jacket and black trousers walked in pushing a cart full of food. Although this breakfast was the most sumptuous I had ever seen, I cared little for it despite my hunger. I would have been happier with sweet chai, the soy paste Mother makes, and hot nan with oil. Such reservations, though, are the luxury of the well fed. The man placed the food on the table and left. As the door slammed, I looked at Hita, who nodded assent, and I attacked the food with both hands. I was scooping yellow eggs onto the bread and pushing it into my mouth. My robe fell open as I did so and food sprinkled and splattered onto my body. I stopped eating with most of the food untouched. Hita watched this uncouth spectacle with a professional detachment that reminded me that the food was only a prelude to the remainder of the day.

A moment later, while sipping tea, Hita informed me that the doctor would be coming to see me later and she asked if there was anything I needed.

'Miss Hita, can you tell me why I am here? When will I be going back to Mamaki Briila?' Hita looked at me, smiled, and answered, 'Don't worry yourself about that for now. It is better that you just think of today. As I said, the doctor is coming soon. Now is there anything you want?' I did not think of asking for clothes but said, 'Miss Hita, could I please have some paper and a pen?' 'You want colors to draw with?' Hita asked. 'No, Miss Hita. I want paper and a pen to write a story with, please,' I said. Hita raised her eyebrows in surprise and replied, 'I will have to keep my eye on you. I didn't realize that you're a smart one. You are the first girl to ever ask for paper and a pen. They usually ask for makeup or a hairbrush or a toy or something like that but never paper and a pen.' Hita looked at me. It was not a pleasant look but not a mean one either. 'I am curious,' she said. 'Are you from an educated family?' I replied, 'No, I learned to read . . . ' I was just about to say, 'when I had TB,' but realized that if I said this I might be sent back to the Common Street immediately. Perhaps she was right; I was cleverer than I thought. I said, 'I learned to read, Miss Hita, from the missionaries back at my home village.' She asked, 'You read English or dialect?' 'Dialect,' I answered. 'Are you from a farming village?' she asked. 'Yes, I am from Dreepah-Jil in Madhya Pradesh,' I replied. The rat-a-tat-tat of questions continued. 'And how long have you been in the city?' By this question she really meant, How long had I inhabited my nest? It is known that the nests are predominantly supplied with girls from the farming towns who are abandoned or sold. I had seen many summers in Mumbai, which are unforgettable because of their unbearable wet heat. 'Six.' 'One more question,' she said. 'So have you written stories for the last six years?' This caught me off guard because I did not understand why she cared. When in doubt, lie. 'No,' I answered. What I failed to appreciate was that one of Hita's responsibilities was to ensure that girls like me disappear off the face of the earth without a trace.

~

Before I left the Common Street I had tied my blue notebook to my back using a piece of string. I did not want to be without my book. Also, I was unsure if I would ever be returning to my nest. The book dug into my back in the taxi but that was a small price to pay. In the hotel room, when I first walked around the Tiger Suite as the blue suit was rifling through his wallet, I had yanked the book out from my back and slid it behind a cushion of one of the armchairs. After this conversation with Hita, I remembered my book's ill-planned hiding place and knew that I needed to move it to a more secure one. The opportunity came almost immediately, when Hita went to the bedroom to call the doctor. 'She's ready now,' I heard Hita say. In a second, I had grabbed the book from behind the chair cushion and slid it under the sofa, where I suspected it would be safe for a while. Hita returned to the main room and told me that Dr. Prathi would be coming to see me soon. She also told me, much to my delight, that there was already paper and a pen in the small desk in the bedroom and that the hotel boy would bring more paper later. Hita said, half chuckling, that she expected to see my story when it was done. I would plan for that.

~

There is a knock at the door. Hita unlocks it with a key she is carrying in the pocket of her white trousers. A hotel man brings in a pile of paper topped with the hotel's insignia: the Royal Imperial Hotel, Mumbai, written in gold. He puts the pile on the table, fishes around in his pocket, and places two pens next to it. Hita gives the boy a coin, which he slips into his jacket pocket before flashing me a flirtatious grin.

Almost immediately after the hotel man leaves, Dr. Prathi arrives. His tummy rolls over his tight belt; I can see that it has stretched the last belt hole almost to obliteration. He has rushed here and he is panting. He dabs his shiny brow with a filthy hanky held in his plump hand. In his other hand he carries a worn black doctor's bag. I can see puddles of sweat spreading under his armpits even through his drab gray jacket. He puffs, 'Sorry I am late; I got here as fast as I could.' Hita steps forward. 'Dr. Prathi, nice to see you. This is not a problem at all — we have all day. Here, this is for you.' She hands him a tan envelope. She continues, 'Please conduct your examination. I have to collect some clothing for her and will be back in an hour or so.' She fishes in her pocket and pulls out the room key, which dangles on the key ring. 'Here is the key. If you finish and cannot wait, lock the door and give the doorman the key. Leave your report over there on the table . . . any concerns at all, please give me a call here this afternoon. If there is anything you need, call on the hotel phone and they can get it for you.' She shakes the hand of the doctor and places the 'thank you' bank note she receives from him in her pocket as she closes the door behind her. I hope she washes her hands.

Dr. Prathi beckons me over to the dining table, where he sits on the chair at the head of the table. He is flowing over it. I sit two chairs away from him but I can still smell him. He turns to me, beaming, and says, 'I think we are going to have a nice time. Well, little girl, what is your name?' 'Batuk,' I say. He pulls a pad of paper and his listening tubes out of his bag. He is also pulling out a shiny metal object I have not seen before, and it clunks as he puts it on the table. He takes a black pen out of his jacket pocket. 'Batuk, what is your family name?' he asks. 'Ramasdeen,' I say. He repeats, 'Batuk Ramasdeen,' as he writes on his pad of paper. He writes in a scrawl. I have not been asked my family name in many years. It has a foreign feel, as if it were someone new I am meeting. 'How old are you, Batuk?' he asks. 'Fifteen,' I say. 'Well, pretty Batuk,' he continues, 'my name is Dr. Prathi and I am here to check that you are healthy so that you can enjoy your stay here, you blessed child.' He waves his arm in the air to indicate something magnanimous. The sweat puddle under his armpit is rapidly becoming a lake.

'First of all,' he says, 'have you had any babies?' 'No.' 'Do you have monthly lady periods?' Amusingly, he points to his groin. 'Yes.' 'How long have you had them for?' 'I don't know . . . a few years.' (You lose a sense of time in the Common Street.) He continues, 'Have you ever had TB or been bright yellow?' 'No,' I lie. 'Do you use these?' Out of his pocket he pulls a rubber-johnny in a red wrapper. Mamaki often told us that if we are ever asked about rubber-johnnies we should say I that we always use them. When a cook wants me to use one, Mamaki, I know, takes an extra ten rupees; even then they are not new but washed from a previous use. The answer to Dr. Prathi is 'Yes, Doctor, always.' 'Good,' he answers, and slips the red wrapper back in his pocket. 'Bituk.' 'Batuk,' I correct him. 'Batuk, I must listen to your heart and lungs now.' He dangles his listening tubes between his fingers. 'Go to the bedroom and jump up on the bed for me and I will be right in.' He continues to write notes and I go to the bedroom to wait for him.

Dr. Prathi walks straight through the bedroom into the bathroom and runs water into the sink. He has taken off his jacket and I can see his back from the bed; his white shirt is drenched in sweat. He hums to himself. He now turns and waddles toward me with his listening tubes hanging from his neck and with the shiny metal object in his hand. He sits next to me on the bed and rolls up his sleeves. He smiles at me and as he does so, he bobs his head up and down like squash plants bobbing in water. As his head bobs, his chin wobbles, his chest shakes, and his tummy quivers. He is like an orchestra of resonating body fat. He asks me to sit up and take deep breaths. He sits behind me and places his hands on my back. 'Deep breaths ... in ... and ... out ... good girl.' Then he taps my back and listens through the hearing tubes. He gets up and says, 'Lie down.' I do. He feels my ribs on both sides and then my breasts — one by one. He presses and moves his hand in circular motions as he feels each. I swear I can see his eyes widening. He then listens to my chest with his tubes. He straightens his back; 'Good,' he says. He then starts to feel my tummy all over, at first pushing softly but then pushing his fingers deep into me. 'Good,' he says again. 'All right, Batuk, open your legs, darling, I need to see down below . . . there's a good girl.'

As he nudges my thighs apart I see the metal object he just cleaned in the bathroom reflect the sunlight. He is advancing it toward me and now pushing it between my legs into Bunny Rabbit's mouth. It is cold and my legs shudder but his arm's weight is behind it and it is pushed inside me. He is muttering, 'Good girl, good girl.' I stare down at his hand and my natural reaction is to tighten my legs on him, but this hurts. He changes his mantra to 'Relax, darling, relax, darling.' As I start to let my legs open and as they stop fighting against him, he presses the metal object deeper inside; as I feel his force pushing into me, it suddenly hurts. I contract my back sharply and let out a yelp. His muffled apology is followed by a repetition of the mantra, 'Relax, darling, relax . . .' but then I feel a deep pain stretching across my tummy. I try to arch my back up, but with the other hand he pushes my tummy down. I wriggle, trying to somehow push it out. He stops, turns to look at me, and says, 'Now you bloody stay still or this will really hurt you! You understand.' I stop moving and nod my head. One thing is for sure, I will not cry for him. He shines a torch at the metal device pinioned between my legs and enveloped by my body. He lays his head onto the bed to get a good look (I consider kicking him but this metal thing prevents me) and then in a second he pulls it out. He straightens up on the bed, and the smile returns to his face. Sweat is pouring off his forehead. 'Now that wasn't so bad, was it?' he says. I say, 'No, Doctor.' 'Good,' he says, 'just one more thing to do.' Before I consider what this might be, he pushes two fingers in Rabbit's mouth. I feel them moving around and twisting and I look up at him staring down at me. A minute later he removes his hand and holds out his wet fingers as if he is waiting for washing to be hung from them. 'Done,' he says. He gets up, walks to the bathroom, washes his hands, and starts to hum again.

I have pulled the robe around myself and cower back as he returns to sit next to me on the bed. He senses my fear of him and smiles at me. His jowls wobble. He reaches for my ankle and speaks as he strokes it, 'Look here, little thing, I'm done and you'll be pleased to hear that everything looks really very good — shipshape.' He continues, 'A couple more questions and then I must write my report and leave so that you can have the loveliest holiday.' He gets out his pad and pen, looks at me, and asks, 'Now, how many men are you with . . . say, in the last week . . . ten maybe?' I look at him. Ten in a week — I would be beaten through to the flesh if I only baked ten times per week. 'No, Doctor.' 'More?' he asks. I nod. Taken aback, he asks, 'How much more?' I answer, feeling the shame I am made to feel, 'Ten in one day . . . sometimes,' I answer. Rubbing my ankle, which at the best of times I would find highly annoying, he continues, 'Little princess, you are now in this lovely hotel, with so many lovely things, a little cuddle for Dr. Prathi would not do any harm and I would give you an excellent report.' I look at him but do not speak. I am the mouse trapped in the snake's gaze.

I say nothing, for there is nothing to say. He grips my right calf firmly in one hand and with his other hand pushes the robe up my legs. He half falls, half climbs, and half rolls on top of me. His weight alone divides my legs under him. His eyes are yellow but he is fat and slow and by heaven he stinks. I try to slide under him toward the floor but his weight traps me. He grabs my left wrist and

176

drives it above my head and pins it there. His grip is so tight that feeling starts to ebb from my hand. 'Listen,' he snarls at me, 'you think I cannot hear your bloody TB lungs . . . you want to get kicked straight back to the street? . . . One word from me and you will be back there in a minute. Now, little girl, I just want a little . . .'

No! I know I am the vessel of all men but he will not have me by his will. I am wriggling and pushing against him with no effect. I turn my head and sink my teeth into the forearm holding my wrist. I tighten my sharp teeth and bite down as hard as I can. My! How the swine hollers. He throws himself backward but he is still sitting on me. Blood is trickling down his arm. His face transforms into crimson and his nostrils flare wide. 'You little bitch whore,' he cries. I smile at him, and *spa!* I spit in his face. By reflex, he raises his bloody forearm high and swipes my face with his open right hand. The sting is agony, but my head will not fall off and I feel a pulsing in my cheek — another bruise. He wipes my spit from his face with the sleeve of his shirt. 'Oh, how you will regret that.' But as he wipes his face, his weight has shifted and I push against his knees and I have slipped free. I jump off the bed and race to the bathroom.

I slam the door shut. My hands are trembling uncontrollably. I am trying to lock the door, but no! The key has gone. I look frantically on the sink. It is not there. Despite the futility, I throw myself against the door with all my weight. *Bam!* — the door flies open and I am driven by its force onto the floor. I am stunned as my head bangs on the stone, but I am conscious. I look over and he is standing in the bathroom entrance, a sweaty mass of flesh spewing torrential anger.

He stomps over to me, his belly trembling with each step, grabs my hair, and lifts me to my feet, drags me to the sink, and pushes my head down into the basin, which is still full of water from when he washed his hands. I breathe out and feel the random, haywire bubbles on my face. I can taste soap. He has me fixed. I try to thrash my head but he has a handful of hair and pushes my face down harder. I draw the disgusting water into my mouth as if I want to breathe it in, but know that I cannot. I relinquish my body, for that is all that is left. All tone washes from my muscle and I start to see gray. 'Ooosh.' He pulls my head out. I gasp for air. I pant. He is pulling the robe off me — off one arm, off the other. I am naked. He laughs and jams my head back into the sink. This time, though, the sink is far emptier than before and I can suck a jet of air through the corner of my mouth . . . if I turn my head just a little bit. He kicks my legs away and pushes my head harder into the sink so that my face is now pressing right down on the plug hole. My legs are floating in the air; I do not even think to kick out. I feel his hand between my legs. He jams his fingers into me and drives them back and forth fast . . . jam, jam, jam, jam, jam. I am pinned, held, bent over the sink, as he pushes his bhunnas into where the metal instrument had been minutes before. His flesh variant is small and barely penetrates compared to the metal and in seconds I feel his poison on my thigh; I guess he did not use the rubber-johnny in his pocket. More enduring, however, is the mixed taste of blood and soap in my mouth.

He raises my head from the sink by my hair and throws me to the stone floor like a vicious roll of the gambler's dice. 'That wasn't so bad now, was it?' he says, and roars out laughing. I hear his zipper and he is waddling from the bathroom. I lie on the floor. There is rummaging around in the main room. I lie still, listening. He is leaving. A few minutes later, I hear the key in the door and then it slams shut and he has gone.

~

There is a specific silence that follows the exit of a person; the air is more silent after a person has left than if he had not been there. There is a tangible silence now. I listen to it while lying on the bathroom floor and my mind starts to disconnect as random thoughts and colors enter it. I think only a few minutes pass before the door is opening again and Hita's voice awakens me. 'I am back, Batuk. Where are you?' I say nothing and lie still. I hear her call, 'Batuk . . . Batuk.' Hita walks into the bathroom with a large bundle wrapped in brown paper. She looks down at me, horror-struck, but does not drop the package. 'What happened to you?' she shrieks. 'The doctor,' I say. Hita's brow furrows in disbelief. 'Dr. Prathi did this to you?' My head nods. 'Don't be so stupid; you obviously fell.' She pulls me up and helps me stand and then she sees me and shrieks, 'He bruised you, he bruised you. You are bleeding. That bastard!' She is white with anger and half carries me to the bed. The lime green bedcover is now smeared in blood. She sits next to me, dialing on the telephone; her finger pounds out the number. Hita is barely coherent. 'It's Dr. Prathi . . . yes, *that* doctor . . . he attacked the girl . . . he bruised her . . . raped her . . . her mouth is bleeding . . . yes,

180

I think that is all right . . . she will be fine . . . she is conscious . . . her arms, her back . . . I will . . . bye.' I can hear a man's voice crackling through the telephone but I cannot hear what he says. Hita replaces the handset and sighs.

~

Hita turns to me. 'Come, let's clean you up! You stupid girl, you didn't need to fight him . . . he is an old idiot! Look at you . . . look at you.' She helps me to the bathroom as I am still unsteady walking by myself. She runs warm water in the sink (the one I was almost drowned in), tests it with her hand, and leaves it running. She turns on the faucets for the bath, and we examine me in the mirror. As I look at myself in the mirror, I reach out to touch me. I feel glass but I know that I am not made from glass. If I were, I would be broken.

My face looks like a garden; a purple flower here and a shrub there. Plant more or till the soil, it will always be a garden.

There is a bruise on my left cheek. Although there is dried blood on my face, there are no obvious cuts on the skin; the blood is either from cuts inside my mouth or his arm. She gently wipes my face with a cloth soaked in the warm water. By the time she is done, apart from the discoloration under my left eye, I look perfect, though my right shoulder is badly bruised and there are bruises from his fingers on my wrist. My back and hip hurt from the fall. She makes me sit on the closed toilet seat, parts my legs, kneels in front of me, and peers between them. She shows a hint of a smile and tells me to get into the bath, even though it is not full yet.

Hita's makeup has rendered the bruise on the left side of my face almost aesthetic, as it now matches a pigmented discoloration on the other side of my face. I love staring at myself in the mirror, and as Hita reassembles me, I do so for well over an hour. I peer into my eyes to try to see myself; stare hard into the black holes but inside of them there is nothing. 'Where am I?' I think. I try to gaze into myself from all different angles and catch reflections of one aspect of me off another aspect. How do I define what exactly I am, as opposed to what reflection I appear to be? The more simple way to argue, though, is that I am as I appear to be now. In this way of thinking, everything is exactly as it appears to be and nothing else. Feelings, the emotions that course through me, thoughts, and the nine senses are irrelevant as I am simply what I appear to be at this moment: a bruised fifteen-year-old prostitute being made up by a woman in a luxurious bathroom.

In this fashion we can similarly look at how others perceive us. I am a straightforward entity because everyone sees me the same way. I make sweet-cake and I am nothing else. I eat, breathe, and move to fulfill that role alone. Others have more complex functions. For example, consider the peddler who walks on his route along the Common Street every day. He carries a basket around his neck that contains batteries, shoes, laces, cigarettes, and other bits and bobs. He tilts his large straw hat to shadow his face so that all you see is a tuft of white hair at the back of his head. The interactions he has with his customers are wholly anonymous; they point, he utters a price, they pay, and he gives them change. This is his appearance to his customers: a straw hat, white hair, and a voice. Appearance one: the peddler. He buys his products from a dealer somewhere, and then he is a customer. Appearance two: the customer. At home, he may be, although I doubt it, a passionate man or even a family man. Appearance three: the father. You see, even the old peddler is a multiheaded animal; with so many different appearances, who is he? Is he the vendor of cigarettes on the Common Street, a customer of others, a passionate lover, or a loving father? When does one role stop and another begin, or do all these roles coexist in a single person? Of course you argue that he is one person supporting multiple swirling roles. However, do you not see that there is an alternate explanation? A man has only one appearance, namely the one you see at the moment of time that you see it; when he sells cigarettes in his straw hat, his sole role on earth is to be a vendor of cigarettes (he is not a father or husband at that moment but only a vendor of cigarettes). Our external reality is exactly what we are at that moment in time; history and the future are irrelevant.

This is the philosophy of the prostitute. I am who I am only at this moment in time; my past does not hang from my shoulders and my future is indefinable and so cannot be a concern. I am nothing else and there is nothing else. As I look at myself in the mirror, it dawns on me again that the tree was correct — all is created for me alone. I close my eyes tight and hear the tree laughing.

~

Up to now, the pace of my new existence in the Tiger Suite has had an unmetered quality;

time has simply been prancing by from event to event. Things were occurring but not in a paced fashion, and Hippopotamus was not keeping record. This was different for me, as hitherto my life was by the clock. When I first started in my nest several years ago, I would become anxious if the clock ticked too many times without my producing sweet-cake. Over time, on the Common Street, I developed an inner rhythm that I tuned my body to, and life followed this beat. In the Tiger Suite, things are different; the clock has stopped. I inwardly watch the second hand and know that soon it will tick, but do not know when. Many times I have prayed for time to stop, but beware of such dreams because should it do so, events will then move along another plane. Without the tick of the clock we are confused and get lost. In order to wait for a bus that never comes, I must sink my roots into the earth to sustain me, but still enter the upper air to see.

~

Time was inching forward in the Tiger Suite like the stooped old man creeping up the Common Street with his walking stick. I lay on the bed staring out of the window, knowing that the next event would follow the last, though when I did not know. As the sky darkened and the sun set behind the building, I got out of bed and walked over to the window. The electric lights on the promenade were coming on and the long lines of light illuminated the streams of tourists, the wealthy, and the beggars. I am not sure how long I watched, but it was quite a long time.

Hita had been in the main room all this time and came into the bedroom. She asked me how I felt ('Fine, thank you, miss') and instructed me to put on my new clothes, which she unwrapped from the brown paper parcel. These were clothes I had only seen on advertising billboards and in the old magazines that Mamaki would occasionally bring us. Hita zipped me into a long red dress that dipped into the breast line and fell away at the back. The trim was gold; it defined where the dress stopped and my skin began. I did not wear an undershirt or brassiere. The fabric of the dress was astonishingly soft. I ran my hand up and down my body, loving the feel of it under my hand and the tightness of it against my skin. My breasts created gentle rises in the fabric. The tail of the dress was split, so that my left leg became uncovered if my leg moved. The shoes were made from black leather, shaped like a fish's body and heeled so high that I could barely walk; in them I became a handbreadth taller. To top it all off, Hita hung white pearls around my neck. I was bouncing with excitement and at the same time toppling over as I attempted to accommodate her. 'No panties, no lines,' Hita said. The makeup, besides hiding the doctor's bruise, made my face look older; I bet Puneet would not have recognized me. Tiger was at a loss for words.

Night fell and the stars sparkled outside my window. Hita ordered dahl and bread for me. It was brought to me by a food man who was different from the one who had brought me the paper earlier. I was hungry. Hita wrapped a towel around me before I ate so that my dress would not get stained, and touched up my makeup afterward. She was pleased with the product of her efforts — as was I. I sensed that the reason for the move from my nest to the Tiger Suite was approaching. Hita paced while we waited in the main room, and I chatted with Tiger.

~

The first indication that the pace of this adventure was about to change was a commotion outside the main door. Then, almost as if by a volcanic eruption, the paired doors of the suite were thrown open. Three men marched into the room, led by the largest. Second in line was the man in the light blue suit (still in the same suit — or did he have many suits exactly the same?). Third in line was the youngest, shortest, and trimmest of the bunch.

It was obvious that the man who led the entrance parade was in charge. He was beaming. Bubba was a one-man force of nature. He stood a head shorter than the man in the blue suit and a foot wider. He wore a gray Western suit; the material was soft and flowed and had delicate vertical white lines sewn into it. His tie was gold and his shirt was ultrawhite. On his left wrist he wore a bejeweled watch plus at least four gold bracelets. On his right hand was a gigantic gold ring with diamonds embedded in it. His right wrist bore a thick gold charm bracelet with what appeared to be teeth hanging from it, along with a host of gold shapes and trinkets. The enormity of his jewelry contrasted (pleasingly) with the delicacy of the white lines in his suit.

His musical movement reminded me of the traditional dancing my cousin used to do for us. She would wear bells on her wrists and ankles so that each limb's twitch carried its own tune and each dance's whirl made its own song. When Bubba moved there was music; he was a song of dangling, clanking, and puffing to the beat of the *whooshing* of thigh against thigh. I loved him from the second I saw him. He was one of those people who could bolt a smile onto your face even if you felt glum. 'Bubba,' he said to me, his hand outstretched. I smiled and tried to skip over to shake his hand, but my left ankle buckled over the shoe and I almost fell. He burst out laughing. Once I reached him, he dropped his outstretched hand and pulled me to him in a tight hug. He wore rich cologne and kissed my cheek. He let me go and turned to the blue suit and said, 'She's perfect.' Raising his voice even louder he called out, 'Iftikhar, Iftikhar, where are you? Look at her. She's here.' Out of the shadow of Bubba, Iftikhar's head popped out. If, at that moment, someone had told me that Iftikhar was Bubba's son (albeit illegitimate), I would have jumped on the table and pretended to be a donkey.

The young man who stepped forth was the total opposite of the patriarch. Where Bubba was generous in physique, Iftikhar was miserly. Where Bubba wore an expansive gray Western suit, Iftikhar wore a traditional (collarless) white narrow suit. Gold necktie for one, no tie for the other. Bangly and clangy, one — soft, silent, and smooth, the other. Effervescent, one — reticent, the other. A clumping elephant, one — a purring gentle household cat, the other. What a pair! The only possible similarity they appeared to have was that they both wore shoes.

The old doorman, his face hidden, gray head ever downcast, gently pulled the doors shut. Despite there being five bodies in the room, there were only three relevant people: Bubba, his son, and I. The man in the blue suit, having been the master mover, was now invisible, as was Hita. Father looked at son and nodded. 'You like her, boy?' His son forced a smile and responded, 'Father, yes, I like her.'

There was a second of silence as if to let the air soften. Unexpectedly, Iftikhar broke the stillness by moving toward the table. He was light and nimble and had a higher-stepping gait than his slim physique necessitated. His movement reminded me of a gazelle. His body was so thin that it merely served as a coat for his skeleton, rather than his skeleton providing a scaffold for his body. Because of his meager physical presence, he looked younger than I suspected he was. I estimated him to be about eighteen. Also, probably for the same reason, his head looked large on his body. It

190

was triangular — wide at the brow, long to the jaw, with thin cheeks. There was an impotent attempt at a mustache below his dead straight and narrow nose.

Sometimes, when I was a child, I would catch lizards with my bare hands; it required enormous inner stillness and explosive release. The lizard's lips reminded me of Iftikhar's. They were thin and pale and rolled over his teeth like cigarette paper over tobacco. Looking closely, I could see that the little muscles of his mouth were taut, which drew his pencil-thin lips inward, as if tightened by elastic. This was a mouth that would hold words in rather than divulge inner thoughts. His hair was a haphazard blob of black. His eyes were his most perplexing feature. They were blacker than they were brown and were framed dramatically by the harsh lines of his face. His eyes held an unwavering stare and I sensed he was somewhere that was 'not quite here.' On first guess, this son of an effervescent, wealthy man might be expected to be the meek recipient of plentitude. Iftikhar was not this at all. His eyes portrayed steel. He was an engine quietly turning over, unconvinced by the exuberance that had seeded him. His eyes were those of a quiet will in waiting, in contrast to his body, which exhibited a jitteriness of immediacy. This was a person you would be foolish to discount or turn your back on.

Iftikhar's voice matched his body. There was tremulousness to his diction and his tone was set high. For a man he sounded shy, hesitant, and effeminate. He said, 'Why is there a pile of paper on the table?' It was a deflecting question that came from a nervous mind. Everyone else looked at my pile of paper too. Hita spoke, 'It is for the girl.' 'For the girl?' Iftikhar said, as much with his dark eyebrows as with his mouth. Hita answered, glancing at me and throwing a wave in my direction, 'She likes to write stories.' 'She does?' Iftikhar said, and cocked his head. He looked at me and was about to say something when Bubba interjected, 'You've got a bright one here, Ifti . . . Anyway, you lovebirds, have a wonderful time. I have business to take care of.' As he said this, he glanced at the blue suit, who silently nodded in agreement, and the two of them turned for the door. As they exited, I heard Bubba say to the blue suit, 'As always, Mr. Vas, you excel.'

❧

The door closed behind them. There was a long silence and both Iftikhar and I looked to Hita as if she knew the next step in the dance.

192

Momentarily thrown, she gathered her wits and said to me, 'Come to the bathroom, Batuk, and I will check your makeup.' I knew my makeup was perfect and followed her to the bathroom. 'Sit!' Hita said to me, pointing to the closed toilet seat. 'I will speak plainly,' she continued. 'You are here to make Iftikhar happy.' She cleared her throat and looked down at the stone floor. 'You will teach him how to . . . how to . . . be a husband.' She cleared her throat again. 'With a woman. You understand?' She held me by the shoulders, her fingers pressing into me. 'You understand?' Never had I truly doubted why I had been taken from my nest to this palace. I understood the impact of time on events and now my current purpose was upon me. I looked at Hita and nodded.

Hita continued, 'You would be a wise girl to make Iftikhar happy . . . If you do, you could be well rewarded, and if you don't . . . well, I am sure you know.' She smiled and I nodded. 'I will be back tomorrow. One last thing: gifts or money or jewelry he gives you — you give to me. You understand, Batuk . . . you understand?' I laughed to myself, as I suspected that Hita was well versed in all the tricks Puneet used to hide little extras from Mamaki. However, the Tiger Suite was much larger than any nest and I was much smarter than Puneet and much, much smarter than Hita. Hita left the bathroom and seconds later, I heard the main door of the Tiger Suite close. The performance had begun.

~

I walk through the bedroom into the main room to find Iftikhar flicking through the pile of empty paper on the table. He turns to me. 'So where's your writing, then?' I lied, 'I haven't done any since I have been here.'

I had written all about my trip here and the grotesque doctor while Hita had been absent. I hid the sheets of paper in the bathroom. By folding the papers lengthwise, I could slide the paper up behind the tubing under the sink and it stayed there, perfectly invisible. What was even better was that I had placed a pen in the crease of the paper fold so that whenever I wanted to write, I would come to the bathroom, pull the paper down, and there was my pen. When I was done writing, I would quickly replace the paper and pen. I have also rehidden the blue notebook, shoving it between the mattress and the base of the bed as deep down as I could reach. I figure that not even the most voracious cleaner will ever find it there.

Iftikhar continues, 'So what would you write about me?' I take the pose of the subservient and look downward. 'I don't really know you.' I tense, as there is irritation in his voice: 'Say how you would describe me!' I hesitate as though I am pretending to think. 'I would say you are nice and well dressed and handsome.' 'How old do you think I am?' he asks. 'Twenty-seven or twenty-eight,' I say. I hear him shifting his weight, but he does not correct me even though I know this is rubbish.

He sits on the sofa, takes the small black control box in his hand, and switches on the television. He is looking at different television channels and eventually chooses football. 'You can sit,' he says. I had remained unmoving, standing in front of him, but now I sit on the sofa next to him, separated by a few feet of space. I clench my hands and my toes and wait.

Which do you think has supremacy, the bus or its fuel? You may say the bus, because it conveys the driver and its passengers over distance. However, it is stationary and useless without fuel. Fuel on the other hand can be used to run another bus or a car or to heat water. The fuel can also be used as a bomb. It is clear that the fuel has the power. Here, I am the fuel and I follow the scent of his fear

195

like a leopard tracking prey.

I remain sitting separately from Iftikhar and watch football with him. I could be watching bread rise for all I care. I do not know the rules or understand the rationale of men dressed in different colors kicking a ball endlessly to each other, only to eventually kick it into a net so that it can be taken out of the net and the process repeated. As I watch I realize that without the ball, there is nothing, just twenty men wearing shorts and wondering what to do for a few hours. It is the ball that has the power. When the game ends (another one will soon start, according to the announcer), Iftikhar turns to me and says, 'Write me a poem.' I do not say anything. I walk over to the table and sit in front of the pile of paper. I close my eyes for a second. My father has come to bring me home from the hospital. I cuddle against his chest, which smells of the fields, and I read. There before me are the streaming verses of Namdev; one verse flows into the next. Soon Father and I are asleep, blanketed in each other's dreams. I take a pen from the desk and write:

My master is a bow of yew
On his arm an arrow rests
It is his command to release
Its flight to feathered nest

196

Listen to my voice whisper:
You
  You are my prize, beyond
  All value on earth, behold
Me

It is a contrived and ugly little poem. I walk over to the couch and hand it to him. As he reads, his upper lip curls in disdain. He asks, 'You wrote this?' To which I respond, 'Yes, sir.' He looks up at me with a gaze as pitiless as steel, smiles, and raises the paper between us. He tears the paper down its middle and then tears it again. As he lets the pieces fall, he watches for my reaction. Does he really think that the paper contains the poem? What a fool he is, for it is the words that contain the poem.

'That is what I think of your stupid poem,' he says. At first, I look down at his feet in feigned regret. 'I am sorry, sir.' Then, I raise my gaze to his. He stands up, the television singing an advertisement in the background, and takes a step toward me. I meet his gaze out of defiance. We stare at each other, our faces a handbreadth apart. Almost as if he cannot think of anything else to do, he spits in my face. There is no malice in this action whatsoever. He spits again. He watches with detached curiosity as his saliva slides down my face. After watching a full minute in silence, he whispers, 'Go clean yourself.' 'Yes, sir.' I subserviently go to the bathroom and wash. The cool water I dab on my face is a pleasant pause and I temporarily become lost staring at myself in the mirror. I turn off the faucet and my consciousness rejoins the present. I return to the main room, which seems smaller than when I left.

'Iftikhar, sir.' It is the first time I use his name and I speak it quietly. 'I am sorry you did not like my stupid poem. It was my first try and I am not a good writer.' He has returned to the sofa and the television. 'Then why do you like writing if you are no good at it?' he asks in a clipped tone. I am standing in front of him. He stares at the television. I answer, 'I do it because I like to put things on paper. I like to see my thoughts because otherwise they are invisible.' His eyes flick away from the television and meet my gaze for a moment. He asks, 'But why do you do something that you are bad at?' I ask him in reply, 'Then, sir, are you good at everything you do?' He thinks and answers, 'Yes.' I am still standing in front of him in my beautiful dress and shining black shoes, a bird of prey. There are torn pieces of paper on the carpet. He continues staring at the television. After a silence, I ask him, 'So what do you do?' This question has baked more bread for me than any other. A man's favorite subject is himself; become his mirror and he will talk forever. He frowns and continues staring at the screen. 'What do *you* do?' he says with a wry smile flickering onto his face. 'You know what I do,' I say, 'but I am interested in what you do.' 'Why?' 'I just am.' He answers without looking at me, 'I waste time at school and work for my father, that fat pig.' I need him to like me and so I take a long stick and poke the snake and agree. 'He seems to be a little overbearing.' 'So you think he's overbearing?' 'Yes,' I say, but I am right, he is a snake, and I have been trapped. 'So you, whore, who screws men all day, think my father, a businessman and financier, is overbearing? Well, let's see if he agrees with you, whore.'

Iftikhar silences the television and picks up the phone that sits on a small table to the left of the sofa. He is watching me with his every movement as he dials. He speaks into the mouthpiece, 'Daddy, hi — it's Ifti.' The snake has me in his coil. Panic seeps onto my face and tightens around my body. He speaks with a sneer. 'I am here with your birthday present . . . I should tell you she has quite a mouth.' I throw myself at his feet. Holding both his feet in my hands I start kissing them. 'Please, please, master, I beg you.' I grasp his thighs in

199

my hands and press my body against him. My breasts press against his knees and I look up at him — an imploring puppy dog. He continues on the telephone, my whimpering in the background. 'Yes, I rather like her. She is more interesting than the last one' (a pause), 'yes, that too' (laughter is followed by a pause), 'yes, yes I will.' He looks down at me, stretches out his lizardlike grin, and puts the phone down. I am desperately grasping his legs. I fold my body over his legs and bury my head between his thighs. As he puts the phone down, he roars with laughter. 'You were terrified I'd tell the fat bastard.' 'Thank you, master, thank you, master,' I say to his legs. 'Now let's see how thankful you are.' He places his hands on the back of my head. The second I feel his hands there, I know that it is I who have him.

He grasps my head tightly and pulls my head up his thighs. He pushes it into his groin. I can feel and see his growing bhunnas through the soft material of his pants. I can size up a man the instant he enters my nest and I am never wrong. I know Iftikhar is as constrained in this area as everywhere else. He is pushing my face down hard over the mound in his pants and I obligingly open my mouth and sing the song he wants to hear. Almost within a second he jams my mouth down over him, pushing as hard as his might can bear. I feel his pulsations on my lips and without tasting the wetness through the cotton, I know his juice is oozing from him. He cannot see this, but my eyes are staring widely into his groin and my mouth is breaking into a smile.

Iftikhar then catches me off guard. In one movement, he throws me off him. I plunge to the floor. I can see the damp spot in his pants from here. He now stands over me. Time slows, but I have no control to move within it. I am watching and cannot move. He tilts his body forward so that his weight rides over his left leg; his right leg draws back. I think of the footballer on television and I become a football. I am watching his foot race to my face. My eyes respond but my body cannot. The contact pain is excruciating. My head is being booted off my body. I am conscious but my head spins, the flesh of my cheek has ripped on his shoe, and I reel in agony, for I am wrong; it is the foot that has power. I scream out as I fly backward and land on my back. He is moving toward me, pivoting on his left leg, but this time my arms pull up to my face and my head folds downward. The impact of his foot on my arms is a new pain. I scamper from him on all fours — a rat — under the table. I cry out; the pain is ripping across my face. I am panting but I can see he is not coming after me. Suddenly Iftikhar screams. I am startled. What right has he to scream? He cannot feel my pain. But then I listen to his noise and it is more a cry that he utters. Within the long, constant howl, I hear a sound I know well: hopeless despair. It is a torrent of misery that spills out of him, and even when his voice becomes silent, the sadness pours forth.

From here under the table I can see his legs. He shifts his weight from foot to foot. His feet are making a decision. I barely breathe. The pain shears across my face. My arms ache. Time passes. He decides; he turns and walks away. The bedroom doors are slammed together and bounce back unshut. I am not moving from here. I do not make a sound. He slams the doors shut again but this time they hold. He kicks at something. Then the noise from the bedroom stops. The television sings another advert.

A long time passes. I am still crouched under the table listening to the television (another game of football). He has not come back in here. I can hear the bath filling. He makes a telephone call from the bedroom but I cannot hear the words. Minutes pass and the bathwater is turned off. I wait and crawl to the bedroom door on all fours, lifting each limb to avoid creating any sound; the carpet is so soft. I listen against the bedroom door. It is silent except for occasional sloshes of water. I get up. I can walk. I try out my body. I am hurt but I can move. I walk to the main door and very gently try the handle. It is locked. I crawl back under the table. I lie here. What? Oh, I know. You don't need to pity me, for you have suffered much worse. You were free. I was also free but a long time ago. Now we are here together. You and I both were wanderers but now here we are together. You need to go to sleep too. Good night, Tiger.

~

Lying under the table, protected by the chairs, I hear a knock at the Tiger Suite's main door. The bedroom door opens and I can see Iftikhar's legs. He unlocks the main door. A tray of food has arrived and he orders it to be taken to the bedroom while he stands (guard?) by the door. He switches off the television in here before locking the main door again and returning to the bedroom. He does not look for me or speak. The bedroom television is on, but an hour or two later it is silenced. I assume that he has gone to sleep.

It is too quiet here. I miss the sounds of the Common Street that have for so long been a part of my rhythm.

Despite the silence, I fall asleep under the table. I half awake with the sunrise as the first sun showers into the room. When I wake up, the carpet where my head has been is stained with darkened blood and my face aches. I need to go to the toilet.

I tiptoe across the main room and silently rotate the door handle of the bedroom. The right door gently swings open. There is a tiny whine of the hinges but not enough to stir the sleeping prince. I inch across the bedroom to reach the bathroom door, which Iftikhar has left open. He is a silent sleeper.

Once I reach the bathroom, I am faced with a dilemma: how best to urinate. If I go in the toilet, I will have to flush it, which will be far too noisy. I cannot climb up onto the sink, and so I decide to urinate in the empty bath. I pull the red dress up over my hips and walk silently up the three stone steps to the bath. I step into it and stand as close as possible to the plug hole and allow my bladder to release itself. The urine is dark and smelly and trickles over the floor of the white tub and down the drain. Once I climb out of the bath, I pull a few pieces of toilet paper from the roll and wipe away any traces of urine, then throw the paper in the trash.

He awakens long before he appears. As soon as I hear movement from his room, I hide what I have been writing behind the cushion of the armchair. I hear him use the toilet, run the bath, and speak on the phone. He switches on some modern music. It must be at least an hour before he comes out from the bedroom. He is wearing a long white robe and his messy hair is wet. I have a strange impulse to go and dry his hair but this urge only crosses my consciousness like a rustling of leaves in the breeze. He walks over to me. I do not fear him but look downward in a show of deference. It is not by design that my eyes fall to the spot on the floor where I had been his football the night before. 'Here,' he says, and thrusts a piece of paper toward me. 'Thank you,' I say as I take it from him. 'Read it,' he says. It is a poem.

My Sword
My sword is made from the finest steel
And flies at every thrust
It parries opposition
To never break my trust
My arm is always forward
My eyes have focused sight
My guard is always ready
I never lose a fight.

His handwriting is far tidier than mine and the penmanship is flowing and without correction, which leads me to believe that he wrote a draft and that this is the final copy. It is the poem of a boy. I look up at him and smile. 'It is brilliant, master.'

I see he is not accustomed to praise, as he smarts. 'Well, it is certainly better than yours,' he says. 'Yes, it is . . . would you teach me to write like you?' I ask. 'Well, first of all, a poem has to rhyme. Yours didn't rhyme properly — it was rubbish.' 'Next time, master, I will write in a rhyme, if I can. Will you let me write you another poem, I beg of you?' He answers, 'Well, I have to go out today with Father. Write me a poem while I am out and I will read it tonight.' I answer, 'I will try my best . . . but please do not be angry if it is not good . . . I will have to study if it is to be like yours.' This angers him; my attempted subservience was in error. He throws his head back and raises his voice. 'If you think someone like you can ever write like me, you are more stupid than I imagined.' I fall at his feet and grasp his ankles. 'Please, master, give me another chance. You are right, you are so right. I will never write as you do . . . I can only try my best.' I feel the tension alter in his feet muscles as he adjusts his body against my hands. I press my head to his feet. He orders me to get up. 'Thank you, thank you, Master Iftikhar,' I whimper. He orders, 'Switch on the television and clean yourself up.' I switch on the television and hand the control box to his outstretched hand. I go to the bathroom, which is becoming my refuge. Iftikhar was not tidy; water has pooled on the floor and wet towels are strewn everywhere. Just before I turn on the bath, I hear him talking on the phone again.

I smile as I lie in the hot water; I have been compelled to write all day long at the bidding of my master.

~

I did not stay for long in the hot water. I dried quickly, put the dress back on, and returned to Iftikhar. He was watching television. I entered silently but he heard and called to me, 'Come here.' I went over to him and sat on one of the armchairs; I did not lean back, as the furniture invited me to do, but instead sat upright. The morning sun was shining in my eyes. I had no sense of his current mood; suffice it to say he was not exuberant. 'Get on your knees.' The hot water had stung my abrasions and my face pounded from the previous night. I knelt in front of him. I knew from experience that the encounter would not take long but I feared the consequence of its brevity. I started to stroke his thighs through his robe and almost immediately saw his bhunnas hardening. I was trying to work out how best to proceed when fate intervened.

Fate is a misplaced retreat. Many people rationalize an unexplained event as fate and shrug their shoulders when it occurs. But that is not what fate is. The world operates as a series of circles that are invisible, for they extend to the upper air. Fate is where these circles cut into the earth. Since we cannot see them, do not know their content, and have no sense of their width, it is impossible to predict when these cuts will slice into our reality. When this happens, we call it fate. Fate is not a chance event but one that is inevitable; we are simply blind to its nature and time. We are also blind as to how fate connects one occurrence to another.

There was a knock on the door. 'Hell,' Iftikhar said, 'breakfast is here.' He stood up and I fell off him. 'Come in,' he shouted. The bulge through his robe was still evident as a gentle shadow in the morning sunshine. The food man entered carrying a tray of breakfast and laid it on the table. He was the same man I had seen the previous day, but this time he glanced at me with dislike rather than flirtation. The seemingly everpresent, ever-invisible doorman sealed me back in with Iftikhar when the food man left; two pickles in a jar.

Iftikhar surveyed the morning's food. I remained sitting, perched on the edge of the armchair. Iftikhar sat at the place that had been laid for him at the head of the table. The plates were made from delicate, almost transparent white porcelain with a gold-patterned rim. The porcelain may have been delicate but Iftikhar was not. He drank tea like a common man, holding the tea cup clasped in his hand rather than by the cup handle as Father Matthew did. As he sipped, he looked at me. 'Turn the television so that I can see it.' He knew that I was watching him eat. I was hungry but I was well conditioned to be so.

At times in my nest I would dream of food, and on each occasion, the dream would contrive for me not to be fed. For instance, in one dream I was behind bars. I saw a feast in front of me in a far-off room, but could not break through the bars despite their being made of paper. In another dream I was swimming in the river when I saw a festival feast being laid out on the river's bank, but however hard I swam I could not reach the bank, even though the water appeared still. In both these dreams my feelings deceived me, for on both occasions I was hungry but did not strive to eat. This is how I felt now, hungry but not wanting to be at the table.

I noticed that Iftikhar drank unsweetened black tea and liked a breakfast of eggs and sausages. For a little man he seemed to eat an incredible amount. He ate like a hungry person even though I knew he could not be. He held his knife and fork in an undignified style, grasping each implement in his fist. He jabbed at the sausage pieces the way I used to stab for fish in the river. He did not take his eyes from mine as he ate, that same steely gaze.

As he wiped his mouth on his sleeve he said to me, 'Now, come over here and finish what you started.' It seemed that my previous dilemma had been postponed rather than canceled. He pushed his chair back from the table, half stood up, and pulled his robe up over his thighs. He sat back down with his entire lower body exposed and parted his legs. I knelt before him and looked ahead between his legs. His bhunnas was hardening before my gaze. It was shorter than my fist. He had a dense patch of curly hair that extended up his upper thighs and stopped at his testicles, which were completely hairless.

It looked as though the artist who made him had dabbed a splash of black paint down there for good measure but had then given up when she realized her painting was displeasing.

I placed my palms on the outside of his thighs again and gently started to stroke up and down. I lowered my head and started to kiss the inside of his right knee. I could taste remnants of soap on his skin. I heard him moan and then felt his thighs contract on my head. He cried out. I looked up and saw that he was emitting his essence skyward. It had taken seconds. They were short little white squirts, six of them. His bhunnas must have been slightly angled to the right, as some of the juice splashed onto his right thigh and then slid downward. The remainder was in my hair. I hesitated and then drove my head deep between his thighs and started hungrily kissing both his legs. I pushed my head into him so that his thighs divided and I started to kiss his scrotum. I moaned, 'Oh master . . . oh master . . . thank you. You are . . . ' Before I could finish my empty applause, he grabbed my hair in his fist, pulled my head up, and threw me away from him. As I flew backward, my shoulder hit the table's edge. My head flicked backward and struck the table with a loud thump. The table shook. The force was so strong that my head flicked back a second time and hit the tabletop again, although the second impact was negligible. I slumped onto the soft carpet and knew to close my eyes and not to move.

Above me Iftikhar shouted out 'Oh shit' repeatedly as a mantra of self-rebuke. First he lightly kicked me with his foot to see if I would respond. I did not. Then he knelt down and shook my shoulder. He placed his hand on my head before quickly removing it and repeating his mantra; I realized my blood must be on his hand. My head was pounding, my shoulder stung, but I was fine. I wanted to be back on the street and I prayed my submission would get me there. Tiger was furious and roared. 'Shh, shh Tiger. I am fine — behave yourself.'

Iftikhar ran for the main door, found that he had locked it, and pounded on it. He shouted out, 'Help — open the door, open the door.' He ran to the bedroom, presumably to fetch the key, but I heard the door unlocking. Iftikhar ran back to the main room screaming, 'Quick! Get Mr. Vas . . . get Mr. Vas.' The door opened. Within moments, a person knelt beside me who smelled of the streets. He gently shook my floppy shoulder and stroked my hair; he whispered in my ear, 'Are you awake, little girl?' I was silent. I opened my eyes a slit to see the white hair on the back of the elderly doorman's head. He was calling to Iftikhar, 'Hurry, she needs a doctor, quickly call a doctor, call the doctor!' Iftikhar was on the phone. In a panicked voice he said, 'Come. You need to come . . . right now . . . there's been an accident with the girl . . . she fell.' Just as he put the phone down, I heard a woman's voice coming from the vicinity of the door. It was Hita. She cried out, 'Oh heavens, oh heavens, not again.' I could feel the rush of air ahead of her as she ran toward me. She knelt beside me and shouted at the doorman to get out. 'But she needs a doctor,' he cried; Hita screamed, 'Get out! Now!' The door slammed shut.

I felt Hita's bony fingers on my neck and then she proclaimed to herself, 'She's alive . . . she's alive.' I felt Hita kneel close to me. 'I feel her breathing. Call Mr. Vas,' she ordered Iftikhar. 'I have already,' he answered in panic. She called in my ear, 'Batuk, Batuk darling. Can you hear me?' She gently shook my shoulder as if to loosen a response from me that was stuck. 'We need to get her onto the bed. Master Iftikhar, please help me.' Iftikhar obviously did not move since she repeated her request, which now sounded more like a demand. I felt three hands under my back and a hand under my head. I was lifted onto the bed. Iftikhar was told to go and get a towel and water. He did not know to warm the water first because its coldness made me start. 'She's moving,' Hita said, principally to herself. 'Batuk, Batuk, wake up, darling,' she pleaded.

The phone next to the bed suddenly rang. This too made me start. Hita answered it. 'Master Iftikhar, the phone. It's for you.' He had left the room, it seemed. 'It's for you,' she called again. Iftikhar used the phone in the main room but it was easy to hear what he said. 'Yes, Father . . . it was an accident . . . she fell . . . she tripped over the carpet running around.' 'And Buddha is a melon,' I heard Hita mutter. Iftikhar's voice was tremulous. 'No, Father, it's this stupid hotel, everything is falling to pieces . . . she tripped over the carpet . . . no, no, she is fine . . . right, Hita?' he called. 'She's breathing,' Hita responded. 'You heard that, Father,' Iftikhar repeated. 'She's fine, Hita just said so . . . all right.' 'Come here,' he called out in the direction of the bedroom. 'Father wants to speak to you.' Hita left my side and walked to the phone, 'Yes, master, yes, master . . . yes, master . . . she is injured . . . on her head . . . it's bleeding and her face is bruised . . . I don't know, she is unconscious . . . I wasn't here . . . yes, she probably . . . yes, a terrible accident . . . yes, she most likely tripped . . . I

214

think we should get a doctor . . . yes, sir, yes, sir, you are right, we should wait . . . Mr. Vas is coming . . . yes, sir. Thank you, sir.

'Master Iftikhar, your father wishes to speak with you again.' I heard Hita return to the bedroom and sit next to me on the bed. It was impossible to hear what Master Bubba said to his son, but he was screaming at him; I could hear it right across the room. This tirade was punctuated by a loud knock at the main door. Hita ran to answer it, 'No . . . no one called the hotel doctor . . . no, everything is fine . . . everyone is fine.' She shouted, 'I said everyone is fine,' and slammed the door shut and locked it.

I lay on the bed for about half an hour when there was another pounding on the door and muffled cries of 'Hita, open it.' Hita sprang from beside me, where she had been intermittently wiping my head. She ran to the door and unlocked it. The door opened. She was slightly out of breath. 'Sorry, Mr. Vas, I left the key in the lock to stop the doorman and the cleaners from coming in.' 'Fine, fine,' he said, 'where is she?' I heard the pairs of footsteps enter the bedroom and felt bodies standing over me. Hita said hurriedly, 'She's breathing fine.'

There was a short pause and I heard footsteps go into the bathroom and the bath being run. In an instant I felt a torrent of cold water drench my head. I sat up coughing and spluttering. Mr. Vas stood at the end of the bed with a tipped-over silver bucket still dripping with water. 'She's fine,' he said. He did not scold me but his look told me that he understood my pretense. He was not wearing his blue suit but rather gray trousers and a white shirt. He was a handsome older man.

I sat up on the bed, my face wet, hair drenched. There they were: Mr. Vas and Hita. Iftikhar entered the room, looking like a condemned man awaiting the firing squad. The firing squad was soon to come.

The silence was broken by Mr. Vas. 'Master Iftikhar, might I please suggest that you get yourself ready, as your father will be here in a minute to go out to the factories. Hita, do you have clothes for the girl? I suggest she wash up. We'll be leaving soon, so there should be plenty of time for you to put her back in shape.'

While Hita had been frantically scurrying around, I was rehearsing in my head. 'A poem,' I groaned. 'What?' Mr. Vas asked. 'A poem . . . Master Iftikhar told me to write a poem today.' Here was the opportunity I could not let pass: a chance to write all day long. I continued, 'He is teaching me to write as brilliantly as he writes.' I certainly had not

216

meant this to be a joke but Mr. Vas burst out laughing. 'You said what? Master Iftikhar is teaching you to be a poet?' For the first time in ages Iftikhar spoke. 'I got an A grade in English last term and Mr. Mitra said I had a gift in composition.' Vas laughed again. 'What Mr. Mitra meant,' Vas responded, 'was that *he* had a gift from your father to give you an A.' Mr. Vas repeated half to himself, laughing, 'A poet . . . ' Humiliation ignited anger in Iftikhar. 'Listen, Vas, you are my father's servant, and when he hears what you said he . . . ' Vas cut him short. 'Listen, Master Iftikhar' (he said 'master' with a sarcastic leer), 'you go right ahead; you tell your father whatever you want. I have a strong feeling that your father will have more on his mind than your poetry right now. All I will tell you is that if you are a poet then I am Elvis! Yes, Master Iftikhar, Elvis reborn as an old Indian!' Even Hita smiled. I stayed impassive as I had a feeling that it would be in my interest to do so. It was a plan well executed. Whether Iftikhar was a poet or not, Hita would understand the need for me to appease him and write the day away.

Vas was still chuckling at his humor (and partially, I think, out of relief that I was still alive), when Bubba burst in. Even from the bedroom you could feel the sonic boom of his entrance. 'In here, boss,' Vas called. Bubba strode in, jangling. Iftikhar was still standing in his nightclothes. I was sitting on the bed with wet hair as Bubba looked me up and down. 'Well, pretty little thing, you seem alive,' he boomed. Vas said, 'Yes, she came to.' 'Good,' Bubba said, 'then no harm done.'

He then walked over to Iftikhar, raising his right arm as he did, and without a moment of hesitation, he struck the boy's head. The power of Bubba's descending open hand could have snapped a cricket bat in two. Iftikhar was completely unsuspecting of this assault and on (jangling) impact was launched under his father's power two feet across the room before landing in a pain-ridden heap. I am sure that his howl was heard in Delhi. I was smiling internally as soon as I realized that he and I would have matching bruises across the left sides of our faces. As I looked down at Iftikhar, bouncing around the floor in pain, you could make out the indentations from Bubba's ring on his face.

'Boy!' Bubba boomed. 'We have to be at the first factory in an hour. Get your clothes on or you'll be going in your sleeping gown. Now get dressed.' I could have sworn that the windows rattled with the might of this final command.

Iftikhar opened the closet in the bedroom, still gripping the left side of his head. He was whimpering while Hita helped him dress. Bubba ushered Mr. Vas into the main room to speak to him privately. I do not think they were aware that I could hear. 'What the hell are we going to do with the boy?' Bubba asked. Mr. Vas answered, 'Well, we could send the girl back, and then we're done with it.' 'But you already paid for her,' Bubba responded. 'It wasn't pricey,' Vas said. 'Say he finishes her — that's going to cost us another hundred thousand.' 'I am a father, Vas. Part of a man's job on earth is to prepare his son for his path, right? My father got girls for me . . . and look at me. This is what you do for your boy. Look, Vas, if he finishes her, he finishes her . . . the trouble is she's a pretty one. You know . . . if I were a few years younger, I wouldn't mind a taste of her myself!' He laughed and slapped Mr. Vas so hard on the back, I could hear the thump. He sighed and then with a voice loud enough to wake the dead, shouted, 'Iftikhar, I am leaving.' Iftikhar, still holding his head, followed his father and Mr. Vas out the door.

~

When Hita returned to me, she appeared contrite; I suspect that, like Vas, she was

219

relieved. I was worried that the bucket-of-water trick might have alerted her to my sham. Instead, I think, she viewed it more as a medical procedure than as a means of removing the cloak from my fine acting. 'You had better get cleaned up,' she said. I obediently went and soaked in the bathtub again, and when I was ready, I came into the main room wearing the bathrobe I found hanging on the back of the door. Hita was sitting at the table, staring ahead. When I entered she looked over to me. 'Are you all right?' she asked.

I smiled at her. 'I am all right.' Hita said, 'So Master Iftikhar told you to write him a poem today. Well, you had better get going then. I am going to get you something else to wear. I have ordered food for you.' Food (bread, dahl, fruit, buttermilk) arrived shortly thereafter, and as soon as the food man left, she gathered up her things. She seemed pleased to leave the suite and locked the door from the outside.

I peered out the window. Light clouds displaced the intensity of the sunshine. I wrote a simple poem for Iftikhar.

Immersion
Immerse me in thy beauty
Anesthetize the pain

Stop my heart from beating
That I never feel again

Come sink within my beauty
Cast away your fear
Hold me close and love me
And let me hold you, dear

Immerse me in thy beauty
Anesthetize the pain
Take from me my fingers,
My pen, my words, my brain

Come sink within my beauty
Cast away your fear
This life is but a droplet
A salty, falling tear

Immerse me in your beauty
Anesthetize the pain
Here is my life. Take it
Make me one with you again.

It rhymes.

⁓

Hita reappeared in the mid-afternoon and interrupted my writing. I quickly shuffled my papers, placing my poem for Iftikhar on the top. 'So you finished your writings?' she said. 'Yes,' I replied. Since the poem lay on top of the pile and my other writing beneath it, I had no fear of discovery even if Hita could read. Under her arm, she carried another bundle wrapped in brown paper, similar to the first. I assumed that it was my next costume. Hita for once appeared relaxed. I smelled a whiff of a particular fragrance on her, suggesting that she had spent some time in a drinking establishment. When she said, 'Let us go and put on some makeup over those bruises and make you all pretty,' I felt that I had already fallen into a routine.

Despite the freedom I enjoyed all morning, the pain across my eyes and deep in my head was constant and had intensified over the day. This cast a net of melancholy over me. It is rare for me to feel this way, but I felt overwhelmed by a blanket of despair. My mind drifted back to the riverbank with Grandpa, the feasts, the feuds with Mother, the fights with my brother Avijit, the smell of dirty perfume on Father's clothes, the conversations I used to hold with Shahalad lying in the back room of the Orphanage, Puneet's whole-bodied laugh, and the jokes we made about Hippopotamus. Who are you to judge if my path is wretched? Judgment is the shadow cast by preconception. You are ignorant of the Common Street and of the raw and wild color that would paint my every hour and splash across my day. But now — here — there is silence, and for the first time I can taste my soul's lament.

~

Hita is skilled with face paint, as a result of which my beauty is restored. She is entirely detached as she rebuilds my face and she steps back in admiration as a portrait painter steps back to admire the image she created. The dress I am to wear is a bright blue with a similar shape to yesterday's dress (I think the store label is the same) except that the back of this dress rests higher up the neck. Before I put it on, Hita stretches a brassiere around my chest, which is obviously meant to accentuate and pad out my as yet quite limited bosom. I slip into the dress and I must admit that the bra does help fill it out somewhat.

We are in the bathroom and Hita is humming as she pins my hair when the main door bursts open. It is slammed shut so hard that the windows rattle. Mr. Vas is screaming his lungs out at Iftikhar. 'You are such a

spoiled waste of space. If I had my way . . .'
Iftikhar's voice is shouting too. 'But you don't
have your way, Vas. You are Father's servant.
You do understand what a servant is? Let me
tell you this, when I take over the Mumbai
factories, I will have you sacked faster than
you can light a match. I will personally watch
you rot in the gutter.' Vas replies with
palpable anger, 'If the boss lets you take over,
don't worry, master, about sacking me. I will
throw myself in the gutter. Believe me,
Iftikhar, he knows exactly what type of weasel
you are.'

Silence ensues before Iftikhar's voice is
heard in its normal high-pitched tone. 'Hello.
Hello. Has my father returned to the office?
. . . Oh, fine . . . It's Iftikhar . . . have him call
me immediately after his call.' The phone is
replaced. Iftikhar says, 'Let's see, Vas, who
Father really trusts. Didn't you know that
trust flows in the blood?' Vas replies, his voice
now calmer and more measured, 'Let me tell
you, Master Iftikhar, I have worked for your
father for more than twenty years and he
knows that I have never put a foot wrong. You
can go to hell.' Iftikhar emits a false laugh.
'Oh, Mr. Vas, we shall see. You forget that
Andy Tandor married my sister and Father
got him the job in the ministry. He is like a
brother to me.' Hita has stopped brushing my

224

hair and we are both listening to the exchange.

Iftikhar switches on the television but immediately the telephone rings. The television is silenced and Iftikhar speaks. 'Father, yes, it's me. Thank you for showing me the factories today, they are magnificent . . . you are incredible . . . I know . . . I so look forward to that, I want you to be proud of me, Father.' Pause. 'Father, I have a serious matter to discuss with you. You know the shipment of cotton we sent to Mauritius under that government contract last year . . . yes, that one . . . did you know that we bought it back from them at forty-five cents U.S. above the original cost per meter? Yes, of that I am sure. Just call Andy at home; he discussed it with me today . . . he is very concerned . . . he can show you the papers. You will be so sorry to hear . . . I was devastated . . . it was Mr. Vas; he's pocketing twenty cents per meter on the sale. I know you needed to know . . . you can ask him yourself; he is here right now.' I hear Vas bounding across the room. He pleads into the telephone, 'Of course, boss . . . this is rubbish . . . of course it is . . . the young master, he's pulling a great joke just to get you going . . . of course . . . of course, call him, we have all the receipts . . . yes, boss, yes, boss . . . of course . . . good night.' The phone is replaced and Vas says in a voice so quiet that I can only just make it out, 'Why would you tell your father that? How could you, you bloody little shit? I have served your family since before you were born. Never did I once skim — not even a penny. I have cleaned up your messes and wiped your nose since you were in nappies.' Then there is noise, a scuffle. Someone has hit someone. There is the sound of a person falling and moaning. I start to get up to run and see but Hita pushes down on my shoulders and we remain in the bathroom.

Iftikhar then says, 'Oh, that's a tragic shame, Vas. You will greatly regret that. You will regret that for eternity, old Mr. Vas. By tomorrow morning you will wish that you had crawled on the floor and kissed my ass . . . now go, Vas . . . I have people coming over . . . go! Oh, one last thing Vas, make sure you screw your wife tonight, because tomorrow I will. When I am done with her, I will send her in my car to visit you in prison, and when you see her little face staring at you through the bars, you will know that I am done with her. Goodbye, Mr. loyal, honest Vas.' Iftikhar's voice is too high-pitched to be menacing and so these threats sound like playground brawn — which sadly they are not. Vas has the last word. 'I don't know which of your father's harlots you slid out of but if I had had my way, I would have shoved you straight back in.' With this the door slams and Iftikhar roars with laughter.

He is still laughing when I hear the phone ring. 'Andy . . . it's Ifti . . . my father will call you in a minute . . . remember what we spoke about earlier . . . excellent . . . exactly . . . yes, twenty . . . see you later . . . yes, I have a real treat for you. We have a lot to talk about.' As the phone is replaced, Iftikhar's laughter subsides as he calls out, 'Girl, where are you?'

~

I do not think that Iftikhar realizes that Hita and I have heard the entire exchange but I suspect his actions would not have been affected anyway. I rush into the main room, with a bobby pin still projecting upward from my hair. 'Where is your poem for me?' he asks, more jovial than I have ever seen him. He is in excellent spirits; his sleeve is smeared with blood. I fetch the poem from the top of the pile of paper that is still on the table and hand it to him. He reads it and looks up at me as I stand before him. 'Well, it is better than your first effort. At least it is a poem this time! But it is quite depressing and lacks any real imagination.' I answer, directing my gaze to his feet, 'Thank you, master, I tried my hardest.' He carries on, 'As I said, it is better, much better, but you have a long way to go,' and with that he raises the paper in front of me and once again tears it down the middle and then tears it into small pieces. The pieces of paper flutter around his feet like leaves falling from an old tree.

I sense that intellectual pursuit arouses Iftikhar. He is certainly the only man who ever asked me to write a poem. As the pieces of paper drift to the carpet, he retains his fixed stare at me. His stare is longer than is necessary to subjugate me, especially since the television is beckoning him. I remember that the only uninjured area of my face is my right cheek, and wonder if he is noticing.

Iftikhar picks up the phone and tells whoever is at the other end to bring him two beers. I am wondering what happened to Hita, having left her in the bathroom. I suspect that she is staying around to ensure my well-being. I remain standing and start to turn away, but then I see his eyes dart upward toward me. He forbids me to leave with a slight shudder of his head. He subsequently puts down the phone. He is watching a soap opera in Hindi. The hero of the soap opera is a doctor whose wife is having an affair with a businessman. The businessman is in turn cheating on his mistress, the doctor's wife, with a younger woman. The doctor is especially handsome and kind (boringly so). As Iftikhar's beers arrive, the doctor's wife is secretly packing her bags to run away with the businessman (who will surely reject her). Iftikhar tells me to bring the beers to him from the table, which I obediently do.

Iftikhar drinks the first beer straight from the bottle in a single draft. He is in a good mood. He takes a little longer with the second beer, and then I understand. He thinks the beer will slow him. As soon as he slams the second bottle down on the table, he gets up, grabs my left wrist, and pulls me to the bedroom. Using my wrist as a fulcrum, he half tosses me onto the bed and stands in front of it. He undoes his brown leather belt and pushes his English-style tan trousers down over his tiny hips, which are smaller than mine. He pushes his trousers off simultaneously with his shoes and then pulls his shirt off over his head. His skeletal form stands before me in socks and briefs. I have to pinch myself not to laugh. 'Oh, master, you are handsome. I think you were so strong and firm with Mr. Vas.' As with all small men, I know that flattery will dissolve him. Iftikhar is about to respond harshly before he changes his mind and says to me, 'You like that, heh! Vas is screwed! I cannot have him around when I take over Father's company. You see, he is far too old-fashioned. It is time for new blood anyway in those ancient offices and time for new offices too.' He laughs at his joke and continues, 'I am really doing Father a huge favor getting rid of that walrus. I bet you he *has* been skimming — that type always does — I have seen it thousands of times. You will see, he will be crawling in here tomorrow begging. Then we will see who the weasel is, eh girl?' 'Master,' I say, 'you are so shrewd. Please, come to me.'

I open my arms and smile, a smile soaked in the dreams of a thousand men. He smiles in response, an ugly S-shaped smile, chiseled from thin lips. I shuffle and sit on the edge of the bed and open my legs. He steps between them. His little candy stick winks at me through the cotton. I start to slide his briefs off over his hips. I only get them a few inches down when I see the first tiny pulsation and then the throbbing as he empties. A dark, wet patch spreads before my eyes into the cotton of his underwear. He stares down as if there were a foreign object taped to his groin. I see anger fill his eyes; it is like watching a glass fill with water. I am trapped by his body. His right arm raises high in the air (I see Bubba in him now). Hita appears in a flash and screams at the top of her voice, 'Master, no.'

With his arm still raised, he almost jumps out of his skin. He looks toward the bathroom where Hita is standing in the doorway. 'Master, master,' she says, 'please don't beat her . . . you want her for the party tonight . . . right . . . I won't be able to find you another girl quick enough if this one is injured.' He thinks about the plea for clemency and then lowers his arm, looks at me with revulsion, and says nothing. He walks into the bathroom, brushing Hita out of the way, and slams the door behind him.

Hita does not look at me or say a word; a moment later the main door locks behind her. Iftikhar runs a bath. I am still staring ahead into the space where Iftkhar's damp patch was a minute ago.

~

Suffice it to say, I am looking forward to the 'party' tonight with the same excitement as one of our pigs who sees Father approaching with his decapitation knife.

Iftikhar bathes for at least an hour before dressing. He dresses in English clothes: jeans, white shirt, and tennis shoes. When he comes into the main room where I am waiting at the table, his mood is difficult to read. His revulsion and anger with me seem to have disappeared. However, he too does not seem to be excited by the party. Tiger, as if a storm is rumbling a jungle away, is also edgy.

Iftikhar calls on the telephone for an assortment of beverages and foods before switching the television on. Thankfully, I have disappeared to him. After a little longer than half an hour, there is a knock at the door and three rolling tables of food and drink are wheeled in. The men in white trousers and black jackets lay it out. There are savory dishes suspended on metal cradles over heating candles; two cakes, one decked in cream and another in chocolate; plates of cold vegetable salads; and fried foods. There is a large tureen of dahl and a tray of breads. There are bottles of different drinks and beers in a tub of ice. For a moment I feel like a hostess and thank the food men, only to receive blank stares in response.

I go and sit perched on one of my favorite armchairs (facing Tiger). Iftikhar has not spoken to me since the moment he was about to hit me and I am thankful for this. I sit there watching him but I am careful that the random glances he directs toward me do not find me staring back at him. I see an angry little man without backbone but there is also an attractive helplessness about him. There is something quite calming about watching a dog flail hopelessly in a fast river before it inevitably drowns. He is powerless in the face of his inadequacy such that it has taken control of him. Instead of being an engine driven by petrol, Iftikhar is an engine trying to drive on vinegar and desperate to understand why he cannot move.

There are loud, young voices outside the room and a *rat-a-tat, rat-a-tat*. Two men swagger into the Tiger Suite with the bounding energy of the young. In contrast, I catch the gentle movement of the elderly doorman drawing the door closed behind them. Iftikhar smiles sincerely at the visitors and gets off the sofa. He hugs them separately with affection. I edge over to the table and stand watching them. Tiger growls momentarily but quickly falls back asleep.

One of the young men is beautiful. He is a head taller than Iftikhar and twice as broad. His body is lean and muscular; his face captivates me. If I were to imagine a modern deity I would not be able to conjure up a figure as well carved as this youth. His cheekbones fall away from his eye line abruptly casting shadows over his cheeks, which are devoid of the plumpness of boyhood. His nose rises from his brow like an albatross and is perfectly straight and narrow. It drops away to form an urgent invitation to his mouth. I want to reach up and kiss his mouth and feel it press on mine; his lips have the fullness and softness of a young woman's. His hair is dark and carefully swept to frame the top of his face with a hint of chaos. His eyes are perfect. They are shaped like headlights in motion, unflawed circles of fire with blazon tails. Fire pours from the hazel-brown wells of his eyes — full of promises never to be kept. Since most of the time he is talking or laughing, there is a gaiety in the dancing to-and-fro movements that his eyes make; I am hypnotized by them. Iftikhar watches me watching him, but I cannot pull my gaze from his. He is delicious and he knows it. His name is Jay-Boy. Jay-Boy is the man of the group to whom the other two defer — he savors this. You would not plunge your hand into a furnace; men like this are dangerous.

The second visitor is called Andy. It is clear that this is the Andy whom Iftikhar spoke to earlier. There is a conspiratorial feel between them that does not so much resemble the love of brothers as the mutual respect of thieves. Andy is round in every way. His face is round, his body is round, his arms, legs, and fingers are round. Even when he smiles, the shape of his mouth forms a curve that parallels the roundness of his face and runs parallel with a neat little mustache that curls over his mouth. He has little round evil green eyes. You could easily miss the darkness hidden in his eyes because when he laughs or even speaks, he squeezes them shut to hide his intent. But as I watch him, I see.

There is high praise for the table full of food and drink. But once this formality is out of the way, they turn to me. Even with the makeup that was necessary to hide my bruises I know I am lovely. I immediately sense that Jay-Boy and Andy want me in different ways. Jay-Boy must possess me as a testament to his manhood whereas Round-Boy must have me as an affirmation of his. I am another food item on the table.

It is clear that the party is not yet complete. They are waiting for someone called Bhim. Although beautiful Jay-Boy may be the focus of attention now, Bhim is the master the others obey. They speak of him as soldiers speak of their captain. They constantly refer to his victories as if they were theirs. They describe with passion how Bhim beat this one or tricked that one. The mode of reference is similar to the way Wolf was described at the

Orphanage; he says — you do. In fact, I get the sense that the party tonight was precipitated by Bhim and certainly the celebrations cannot start without him.

As the three boys sit on the sofa together and watch television, there is warmth and a palpable connection between them. Whether it is the herding of lambs or the affinity of boys, I do not know. The three of them sit on the sofa, jostling their bodies against one another, nudging one another's shoulders, and slapping one another's legs and arms. They entangle their voices in the same way, laughing and talking; one is always trying to outdo another. In an instant I am drawn back to the dining table with my brothers, who were always poking one another, fighting, and laughing. You could not help smiling as you watched them. Tiger and I watch these three boys and we both smile. I am puzzled by our ability to connect distant moments of time as one. I pull the laughter from so many years ago to the present and feel the happiness that I understand only now that I miss.

~

The three boys watch cricket, principally at Jay-Boy's request (I know that Iftikhar hates cricket). Jay-Boy and Iftikhar sit drinking beer straight from tall green cans and Andy is drinking a tea-colored drink poured from one of the bottles at the table. Their words are already slurring and their laughter is somewhat uncontrolled; they are not seasoned drinkers.

The laughter is silenced by the telephone. 'Father,' Iftikhar says with excessive and insincere enthusiasm, 'it is wonderful you called . . . I am.' Iftikhar is obviously interrupted and his tone changes. 'He is here,' Iftikhar says seriously and indicates with his hand to Jay-Boy and Andy that they need to be silent. 'I agree, Father,' Iftikhar says. He is looking at Andy as he speaks and now he is smiling at his co-conspirator. 'I did not want to tell you at all, but I thought it was my duty . . . to me, Mr. Vas is like an uncle . . . I know, I know . . . he used to rock me on his knee. Father, may I ask you, now that you have discovered that Mr. Vas has been stealing, what will you do?' He raises his eyebrows and smirks at Andy, who grins in response. 'Father,' Iftikhar protests, 'I beg of you, please, please do not sack him. I am sure there is another job he could do, say in one of the warehouses . . . He has a lovely wife and they have children . . . oh, I understand . . . I have a lot to learn from you. You are right, of course. If others saw you being lenient with a thief, there would be no stopping them. I will be sorry to see him go, though. Father, when will you tell him? Right now, are you serious? . . . I understand. I have so much to learn. Goodbye, Father . . . really it is Andy you should thank . . . yes, I will . . . he feels sad too as he knows how much I love Mr. Vas.' They smile again. Iftikhar carries on. 'A few other friends are coming over too . . . yes, Father. Yes, she is. She is working out fine. Thank you . . . we will. Goodbye.'

As he hangs up, Iftikhar punches repeatedly in the air with his right arm and Andy starts clapping like an imbecile. Jay-Boy is eyeing me. Iftikhar and Andy jump up and perform a little jig in front of the sofa. They toast each other. 'Ifti,' Jay-Boy says, interrupting the jubilation, 'can I take your little toy here for a quick test run in the bedroom.' Iftikhar's guard is down and he hesitates. Jay-Boy gets up and advances toward me but Iftikhar stops him. 'Jay-Boy, you'd better wait until Bhim gets here. He is bringing over some girls too . . . you know what he's like.' Almost immediately, there is a loud knock at the door, from the other side of which I can hear giggling.

★ ★ ★

Enter Bhim, enter Bhim's attendant, and enter two girls.

Bhim is of medium height and has unremarkable features, neither attractive nor ugly. You would walk past him in the street without noticing him except for the sense he emits of being in charge. He does not use extravagant mannerisms or a loud voice, but you can sense his authority. He wears a smart black cotton jacket, a white T-shirt, and jeans, and he is followed by a dog. His dog is a head shorter and broader than he is and is dark skinned, with a somewhat squashed face. The dog's eyes are hooked on Bhim and he says nothing; short of a wagging tail, he would actually be a dog. As Bhim takes a seat on the armchair nearest the door, his dog takes a seemingly natural position standing behind his left shoulder.

The two girls are much older than I am and clearly are attending the party on hire. Their paymaster is Bhim and they accord him the attention he has paid for. One girl, wearing an orange T-shirt, is very full-busted; this is her principal attribute. Her T-shirt is dramatically stretched over her bosom and has the word 'Bebe' written across it in shiny stones. Each gigantic breast is larger than my head. I am impressed that the parchment-thin material retains her breasts at all, as they are poised like wild cats to leap from it. Her face is ugly and you can see where she plucks her chin hairs. She is wearing tight blue jeans that cover her generous bottom, and her black-heeled shoes are similar to the ones I am wearing. Her overall appearance is of a massive pair of orange breasts.

The other girl is quite lovely; she has long, flowing, shiny black hair, a well-proportioned body, and beautifully painted lips. She has a black spot on her left cheek just above her mouth, which I suspect is from ink. She is probably a little too beautiful, as this intimidates men even when money has already been exchanged. She is wearing a rippling silver top that falls away completely at her back so that her skin is revealed. Her back is so smooth and without blemish that you just want to touch it to see if it is real or porcelain. She is wearing tight white trousers, no underwear, and brown leather boots to her mid-calf.

The girls, like me, are not introduced by name. When I was in my nest I often used to think that I had lost my name altogether. I had become an anonymous unit without any function; who names a broom or a table? The girls and I were objects and as such unnamed.

The pet dog is dismissed and leaves. He is the only one to address Tiger, who reciprocally bids him farewell.

The beautiful girl serves Bhim the same drink that Andy has and then the women help themselves. They do not acknowledge me. The party is beginning. Jay-Boy is still eyeing me and now that Iftikhar's authority to deny him is muted, he takes me into the bedroom. He is easy to please and I am easy to possess.

He returns to the group and I wash myself quickly in the bathroom so that I can steal a little time to write. As I leave the bathroom, the ugly girl is reminding Bhim of long-forgotten days of feeding from his mother's teat. He is lying on his back on the bed as she straddles him. She is feeding him her left breast by pushing its nipple into his mouth using both of her hands. He is clothed and she is naked. He watches me walk through the bedroom. She, again, does not acknowledge me.

In the main room, Jay-Boy is sitting in the armchair with the pretty girl on his lap. Iftikhar and Andy are together on the sofa. They are watching a music show on television. Iftikhar and Jay-Boy are smoking. Jay-Boy smiles when he sees me and calls over to Iftikhar, 'You lucky man, she is quite a fox.' Iftikhar answers in kind, looking at me fleetingly as he speaks. 'I rammed her the whole weekend. She cries for more all the time; she really loves it.'

Jay-Boy interjects into the stream of fiction, 'I think Andy should take her for a turn.' The pretty girl says, looking playfully saddened, 'Oh, come on, Jay-Boy, I told you I want Andy.' The pretty girl is smart as she knows how hesitant and obedient Andy would be; an easy student. Andy blushes visibly and Iftikhar's goading makes him blush more. 'Andy wouldn't know which end to start. I'll tell you one thing, Sheenah, his princess wife, doesn't give him head — that's for sure. Right, Andy?' Andy meekly responds, 'Ifti, she's your sister.' There is an uncomfortable hush broken only by Tiger's laughter.

Bhim enters from the bedroom. 'What, Andy gets no head? We'd better put that right, right, Andy?' Iftikhar adds, 'That's if he can get it up.' Iftikhar, Bhim, and Jay-Boy burst into raucous laughter at Andy's expense. Andy reddens from embarrassment. Jay-Boy calls over the laughter (I sense with a sprinkling of malice), 'Ifti, take Gee-Gee to the bedroom, she really wants you.' The beautiful one, obviously called Gee-Gee, interjects. 'No! I told you I want Andy,' she says, playfully pouting her lips at a still red-faced Andy. Iftikhar responds, 'I had the little bitch there,' pointing at me, 'twice before you got here. I also want to see Gee-Gee on Andy.' I am not sure whether

Bhim sees through Iftikhar's front and so speaks mockingly or whether he believes him, but he says, 'Ifti, I knew you had the rocks . . . I'm going to try your dolly, then . . . if she can handle it.' You see: 'your toy,' 'your dolly,' 'the little bitch'; that is how they refer to me, but never as Batuk.

As Bhim beckons me to experience 'the roller coaster,' as he refers to himself, I glance over my shoulder at Iftikhar. There is such a delicious flood of dejection emanating from him that I hold his sad stare for a second longer than I intended — just to relish it. Suddenly, though, I feel a prick of sadness because I remember the moment that Wolf took me from Shahalad. The difference is that then I longed for Shahalad in a way I had never experienced before. Iftikhar's humiliation is my yearning now.

In the bedroom, Bhim is surprisingly gentle. Young men generally use physical strength to communicate their potency. I appreciated long ago that this reflects a lack of confidence and immaturity. The overreliance on the physical renders them poor lovers, which is why, I suppose, their wives reject them. Bhim is different. He wishes to emulate an exchange of fondness between us. I see this more commonly in an older man, who oftentimes I suspect is married to a woman no longer capable or interested in providing affection. I can become a daughter to these men and provide them with the forbidden love of the powerless. It is rare for a young man to want affection from me, and it is tiresome because I have to extend my dramatic skills beyond the most simple of dances.

As we lie opposite each other, Bhim smiles and strokes my hair. He wriggles closer to me so that he is a handbreadth from me. He strokes my bare arm and smiles. 'So,' he says, 'Master Iftikhar is wearing you out.' I smile back at him and respond, 'Yes, I am tired,' which is true. I have nothing to gain by affronting Iftikhar. It strikes me that I have not gained anything by being brought here; I miss the sounds of the city, the others, and even the heat. As I lie here on the soft bed in the cooled bedroom, I feel the tiredness for the first time and I want to fall asleep. Bhim smiles at me in a way I cannot decode; at its most simple it is a polite smile. He puts his arm around my waist and pulls me closer to him and now strokes my bottom and my thigh. He rubs my dress higher up my thigh so that my entire leg is exposed and I feign pleasure; if I had my choice I would slice his hand from his body. His grip is a mixture of strength and boniness, and with his hand now on my exposed buttock, he leans over me to kiss my neck. This is standard for many cooks. I coo for him and think about how sweet the mango was yesterday. He leaves saliva on my neck, which feels cold as it dries. I love being able to be clean. I will wash him off very soon. 'Your lips are very gentle,' I say.

'Why don't you get that pretty dress off?' he whispers in my ear. I oblige. He then fiddles a little to remove the bra and I feel a little depleted, remembering the huge offerings of the ugly girl. I realize that I am still young but know that I will never become that generous in my body. He starts to kiss my breasts and then he pushes his hand between my legs. I lie and stare at the bathroom door. I am thinking to myself that one day I would like to write a story about the tiger. I call out 'Tiger' with my undervoice. Bhim's teeth nip my left nipple and I flinch; I wince in feigned pain, as many cooks love to hurt me. He carries on kissing my breast. I think of Tiger asleep in the next room.

Bhim says, 'Oh, you are all wet for me, baby,' as he wedges a hand between my legs. 'Yes. You are very handsome,' I say. Has he forgotten that I have Jay-Boy's spill in me?

'Wake up, Tiger. I am going to write a story about you one day. I need you to tell me about your mummy and daddy and the other cubs. Tell me about the jungles you ran through and all the deer you hunted. Wake up, Tiger!'

Bhim is kissing me between my legs on Bunny Rabbit's mouth. Can he taste Jay-Boy? I find this thought pleasing and rub his hair as he licks and partakes of Jay-Boy. He wants me to roll on top of him. He wants me to stare down at him as I move on him. I oblige. The bhunnas is not excessive in size and I pitch to and fro. He closes his eyes, only to open them to ensure that I am looking at him, which I am. How you pace a man is important; too fast and he deflates (Iftikhar's limitations were not by my design), too long and he burns out. It is like baking a cake. I am concerned that since Ugly Girl has just worked him, Bhim will take forever. I need not have worried; with seven or eight twists of my hips as I descend on him, Bhim gives himself to me. He is delighted with his sweet-cake. I smile at him amorously and politely excuse myself. I close the bathroom door shut, pull my bundle of paper from behind the sink, turn on the bathtub faucets, and write. I feel a growing desperation to melt within my ink.

The room is steaming up. There is a violent knocking at the door which then flies open.

Plain white paper

I will never be able to explain exactly how this sheet follows the last. Words come to me with far greater effort both mentally and physically. I sit in bed with my back against a steel frame. On awakening, I did not immediately realize that I was in a hospital, probably because of the medication, which I think is also making me feel woozy and sick. The pain is returning and so the medication must be weakening.

My memories of the events that brought me here are, like my words, only sketchy. It has taken me a couple of days to patch together the events that took me from the bathroom to this hospital bed.

The police sergeant is interested in my account of what happened and has asked me to write down everything I can remember. He was dumbfounded when he learned that I could write. He went and got my blue notebook from under the mattress in the Tiger Suite and took away all my other writings. Lying here, I have been told that I

247

have nothing to fear from the police. I think that I may have much to gain by aiding them; the doctors will certainly not forget me with the police coming every day to talk to me.

⋆ ⋆ ⋆

As best as I can recollect, here is what happened.

The urgent knocking on the bathroom door was only Gee-Gee, the pretty girl, who had to clean out Jay-Boy from inside her. He had apparently dealt with her on the armchair in the main room while I had been baking with Bhim. She agreed with me that he was easy to please. I remember we giggled like schoolgirls after I told her how amazingly beautiful I thought she was. She was naked below the waist, which made the moment between us even more sisterly. 'So what are you doing in here?' she asked. 'I am writing,' I answered after some hesitation. 'What are you writing?' I showed her the sheet of paper I was writing on and the whole pile of my writing that rested on my lap. She took hold of the pile and fanned through it in silence. The sheets of blue script blurred into one; I knew she could not read but did not want to offend her. 'It is just my silly thoughts,' I say. She looks at me with a pure smile of sunshine

and says, 'You are so pretty and so clever . . .'
She fans the pile of paper again, looking at it
in awe. She asks, 'How old are you?' 'Fifteen,'
I answer. 'Did you come from a brothel or are
you private?' 'Brothel,' I say. I am ashamed to
tell her that I come from the Common Street,
as it is the lowest level. Girls from brothels
are far higher, and private girls the best. 'How
about you?' I ask. 'Private,' she says. I am not
surprised as she is so beautiful and poised.
She would have known the foreigner hotels
well. 'You make good money?' she asks.
'Mamaki keeps my share for me for when I
am older.' Gee-Gee bursts out laughing. 'Oh
darling, are you being serious?' 'My name is
Batuk,' I say. She looks at me, pauses a
second, and she understands, for she too is
nameless. She says, 'Batuk, you will never see
a rupee of that money! You need to get out
while . . .' She is interrupted by Bhim, who
has silently appeared at the bathroom
doorway. 'Get your asses in the main room,'
he says.

After issuing his command, Bhim halts. He
looks at the pile of papers in Gee-Gee's hand
and pries them from her. I watch him and
hold my breath. The second I see his eyes
scanning the lines I know he can read. 'No,' I
scream and instinctively throw myself at him,
grasping for the papers. What a terrible

mistake. He pushes me back. I come at him again but he kicks me to the floor with savage thrusts of his right leg (not so gentle now). He takes a couple of steps backward out of the bathroom, brandishing the papers high above his head. 'Now what is this?' he asks. 'It is just my silly scribbling,' I say beseechingly to him. 'Please give them back to me. They are just my silly stories.' I run at him for the third time but he sees me coming and swats me away with the back of his left hand. He shouts, 'Jay-Boy, get in here right now.' Jay-Boy runs into the bedroom and Bhim tells him with a huge grin on his face, 'Hold her back.' Bhim is the beggar who was just handed a glass of water to find it full of diamonds. Jay-Boy grabs me round the waist, twists me away from Bhim, and I start kicking. Gee-Gee slinks into the main room. Jay-Boy takes my wrists and pins them against the bedroom wall; he presses his body into mine so that I am stuck. I stop struggling altogether.

Bhim sits on the bed and reads. I can hear the television in the main room but nothing else. Bhim starts to laugh. 'You have got to hear this,' he says to no one in particular. He starts reading to Jay-Boy in a melodramatic voice and I start to cry.

250

I placed my palms on the outside of his thighs again and gently started to stroke up and down. I lowered my head and started to kiss the inside of his right knee. I could taste the remnants of soap on his skin. I heard him moan and then felt his thighs contract on my head. He cried out. I looked up and saw that he was emitting his essence skyward. It had taken seconds. They were short little white squirts, six of them. His bhunnas must have been slightly angled to the right, as some of the juice splashed onto his right thigh and then slid downward. The remainder was in my hair. I hesitated and then drove my head deep between his thighs and started hungrily kissing both his legs. I pushed my head into him so that his thighs divided and I started to kiss his scrotum. I moaned, 'Oh master . . . oh master . . . thank you.'

Jay-Boy hoots like a baboon. 'How about this?' Bhim says, and reads aloud,

I sense that intellectual pursuit arouses Iftikhar.

'Wait until his father hears that. Iftikhar failed so many exams this year that even Bubba can't afford him anymore.' He and Jay-Boy burst out laughing. I feel Jay-Boy's body bounce against mine as he laughs.

Bhim carries on and says, 'You have got to hear this . . . '

I shuffle and sit on the edge of the bed and open my legs. He steps between them. His little candy stick winks at me through the cotton. I start to slide his briefs off over his hips. I only get them a few inches down when I see the first tiny pulsation and then the throbbing as he empties. A dark, wet patch spreads before my eyes into the cotton of his underwear. He stares down as if there were a foreign object taped to his groin.

'It looks as though math and chemistry aren't the only things our friend Iftikhar fails at.' They are doubled up with laughter. Jay-Boy repeats '*little candy stick*' in hysterics.

Bhim walks into the main room brandishing my papers. Jay-Boy follows, half dragging me; he has me tightly gripped around the waist. I am kicking and screaming, 'No, no, no.' As we enter the main room, Iftikhar looks around. Initially, Ugly Girl was concealed by the back of the sofa but now I can see her kneeling in front of Andy, who has his trousers crumpled around his ankles and his underpants stretched across his knees. Her head is bobbing up and down on Andy's groin. She does not miss a beat even when the three of us enter (she is a professional). Bhim starts to read the same passages with the same theatrical tone. Ugly Girl now stops and resorts to swirling hand actions on Andy; she is all ears. As Bhim finishes the first excerpt, Iftikhar looks over at me; I am now flaccid in Jay-Boy's arms. Even though I cannot think of anything to say, I know it will not make a difference. What is more, I feel no regret. The second piece that Bhim reads out roots Iftikhar to the spot and the third piece annihilates him. I see his entire being tighten like a drawn bow. Then he snaps. *Twang!* He leaps for me. Jay-Boy sees him move and spins me away from Iftikhar but does not release me. Bhim is doubled with laughter and Andy is smiling.

Iftikhar has spun to the other side of the room and screams so loudly that Ugly Girl drops Andy's bhunnas, which flops down like a fallen battle standard. Iftikhar yells, 'Shut up. Bloody shut up, Bhim.' Bhim turns to him. 'Heh, Ifti, don't shoot off your mouth at me.' There is a moment's silence before Jay-Boy and Andy get the joke and burst out laughing; Ugly Girl got it right away but knew better than to laugh. I watch Iftikhar implode. Then he turns his gaze to me, half shielded by Jay-Boy's body. Iftikhar says, looking straight at me, 'So you all want to see me fuck her, and hear the bitch scream as I do it? Is that what you all want?' Bhim answers, 'Will I miss it if I blink?' Iftikhar turns to him and in naked hatred spits the words, 'I said, do you want to see me fuck her? Yes or no?' 'Iftikhar, I would love to see it — perhaps during a TV advert,' Bhim says.

~

Iftikhar's voice is loud but controlled as he speaks over his friends' laughter. 'Boys, pin her down on the floor for me. She is going to scream to hell when I am through with her. Bitch,' he says as he looks over to me, 'you will feel my love for eternity.' Iftikhar is past the point where he can regain himself. He topples the low glass table aside from where it was located in the center of the sofas and chairs. The sound of the glass breaking is deafening, as if to invoke silence from the onlookers, who no longer speak or laugh. Iftikhar says to Jay-Boy, 'Bring her over here.' Jay-Boy hesitates and Iftikhar tosses his head and screams, 'I said bring that little whore over here.' He obeys and pushes me toward Iftikhar, who stands where the table has been.

I do not resist. I look within Iftikhar's eyes and see where the rats have gnawed away at his inner remnants. He walks up to me, holding my gaze, and in one action punches me across the face. I do not lose consciousness but the impact and the pain disorient me. I shake my head, look within, and laugh.

I feel the happiness that the insane feel when they are released from the confines of the ordinary world. 'Get her on the ground,' Iftikhar says. 'Andy, sit on her chest.' Andy replies, 'Ifti . . . this isn't a great idea. We all know the little whore made it up. You told me you fucked her crazy, like ten times . . . we don't need to see you . . . right, Bhim?' he asks Bhim, almost begging. There is silence. I notice that the girls have disappeared. Bhim is silent for several seconds. He eventually says, 'Actually, Andy, I do want to see Iftikhar fuck her. I just hope I don't sneeze and miss it.' Bhim continues with a soft smile on his face, 'Andy, sit your ass on her chest like he told you.' I start kicking like a crazed animal as Jay-Boy pushes me down, in part by kicking me at the back of my right knee. Andy lowers his globular mass onto my chest so that all I can see is his back; there is sweat soaking through his shirt and glistening on the back of his neck. These boys are now a herd.

Iftikhar says, 'Jay-Boy, Bhim, take a leg and

spread her wide.' Jay-Boy kneels below my feet, grasps my ankles, and spreads my legs apart. I start clawing at Andy's back. He cries out. Bhim grasps my wrists, drags them over my head, and sits on my arms. I feel my dress pushed up my legs. Then I see Iftikhar standing between my legs. I feel him pushing his shoe onto Bunny Rabbit's mouth. Eyeing me, he says, 'So, little whore, you think Iftikhar can't fuck you, huh?' I say loud enough for Tiger to hear, 'Ifti baby, you couldn't fuck a cabbage.'

I see Iftikhar's leg go back and I know what is coming. Nothing could have prepared me for the feeling as he kicks Rabbit's mouth. My body explodes. I am barely conscious; noise fills my head. One of the boys, although I cannot tell which, says, 'Well, you still haven't fucked her.' In seconds that traverse many planes of time, I see Iftikhar walk over to Tiger and lift one of the ornamental swords off the bracket below Tiger's face. He carries it over to me. Iftikhar wears the same expression on his face as he did the first moment I saw him: steel resolve.

I feel the tip of the shining sword against Rabbit's mouth. Just as the steel touches me, showers of electricity flood through me. I spasm in pain, and arch against Andy's weight. The boys are screaming at him but

Iftikhar yells them to silence. I see his face stare down at me over Andy's back. I see him place the top of the sword handle against his stomach. The tip pushes against Rabbit's mouth and the pain alone rips me apart. He stares at me and says, 'Now who's fucked, Batuk.' It is the first time he has spoken my name. Tiger roars for the heavens to come to earth and then I feel nothing.

~

The nurse told me I was in the newspaper, which amazed me, and I asked her to read what was written in the article as I do not speak English (except for a few choice phrases). I could hear the hesitation in her voice as she held up the newspaper. I was pleased for the company anyway. The actors around me appeared to be the hopeless, the moaning, the wailing, and the half dead. This hospital was more crowded and decrepit than the chicken coop I had been in when I was a child, and these patients were older and more helpless. The place reminded me more of the Orphanage, a receptacle for human garbage.

The stage was colorful: the deep red of blood-stained mattress covers and towels, the yellow of urine, some fresh and some years old, the shades of gray of my fellow patients, the orange of iodine, and the pale blue-brown mixture on the walls where there was less paint than more. There was an opera of sound too: the jingle-jangle of the steel carts, the rustling of the uniforms, the voices of medical hierarchy, and the sublime chorus of the patient choir, some singing their finales. The smell was an invisible but essential part of the atmosphere, a blend of ammonia, decaying human flesh, and unclean mouths all simmering together to form the distinct odor of death.

The nurse started by clearing her throat. She read slowly, as she was translating the English for me.

Carnage in luxury hotel. Today police are investigating the massacre of four young men found slaughtered in the penthouse suite of the Royal Imperial Hotel, Mumbai. One of them is the eighteen-year-old son of Delhi billionaire Purah 'Bubba' Singh. Chief Repaul stated that all available leads are being explored to find the guilty ones.

She cleared her throat again.

Bubba Singh was not available for comment, although a source close to the family stated that Mr. Singh's son was having a party after successfully completing his school exams. He was planning to enter the family business. The tragedy for Bubba Singh was compounded because another of the victims was his son-in-law, Oojam 'Andy' Tandor, who leaves a young widow. Sources close to the prominent family revealed that she is pregnant and expecting in the spring. There was only one survivor. A maid, Hita Randohl, discovered the bodies and called hotel security. She is currently being questioned intensively by the police.

The nurse looked up at me. 'That's you they're talking about.' I smiled. Here in this newspaper, just as when all my bakers return to their wives, I had become anonymous, 'one survivor.' She continued:

Police were called to the luxury hotel, which has hosted many celebrities and stars such as Mahendra Singh Dhoni, Margaret Thatcher, U.S. senators, and the Police rock music group. There were reports by hotel guests of loud music and boisterous behavior during the entire evening. A major disturbance was first reported to hotel, security around midnight. Mr. Ghundra-Chapur, the manager of the hotel, reported that hotel security guards responded immediately to the maid's emergency call. He said that when the guards entered the luxury suite and found the bodies, the police were immediately called. 'This is a terrible tragedy, and our thoughts and prayers are with the families,' Ghundra-Chapur said.

In Chief Repaul's statement, he reported that 'the four young men were killed by violent means.' Although he denied gunshots, he would not reveal the cause of death at this time. Hotel guests confirmed that they did not hear gunshots. 'Just loud music,' one of the guests, Mr. Peter Seville from Connecticut in the USA, said.

The deaths have already rocked the Mumbai business community. 'No resources will be spared to find the guilty,' Chief Repaul stated.

It was obvious that there was more in the paper, but the nurse shut it. She shouted for an elderly orderly to bring her a towel, and she wiped my sweating brow with a damp cloth and disappeared.

The last few days have not gone well. Whenever they withdraw the pain medications, the pain becomes excruciating. I can still feel Iftikhar's shoe and the sword's steel, but when the medications are given back to me, I see gray and sleep. I am having more fevers today. The nurse pushes several types of cream into my bottom to make me go brown, but I cannot go. The doctor in his white coat shook his head while writing on my board earlier; his silent gaggle of attendants looked downward. I even sense that the nurses are giving me less attention, as if their time would be better invested elsewhere. During my high fevers they make sure the old attendant wipes my brow, and when the fevers subside they say, 'Try to drink some broth.' I feel tired all the time. When I am not feverish, I must write. All that is left of me is ink.

The policeman has come to see me twice more to ask if I remember anything else about that night — but I do not. The policeman is nice. He has read my writings and looks at me with pity. I never asked for his pity but he gives it freely. I sense he is desperate because today he was asking me the same questions as before but with greater intensity. He asks me a lot about Mr. Vas. 'Was he there?' 'Did you see him at all that night?' I have already said no many times to these questions. Now I just shake my head to save the energy of speech. I smile and remember his light blue suit. I know the policeman wants me to say that I saw Mr. Vas that night but I did not. Mr. Vas brought me here to the hospital, he tells me.

Why did Mr. Vas pluck me off the street, clasp me in his arms, and gently lay me on this hospital bed? I have no idea. He has not been to visit me.

The policeman asks me again if I know who carried out the attacks and again I explain that Tiger did.

In my fever I see circles of different colors and different sizes moving forward and backward and to the side — zooming around and sometimes still. The world is circles — or are they hats? — that connect this to that in invisible moving patterns.

Last night was the worst but I will not write of it. There is only a little ink left.

~

Today there is great excitement in the hospital room because the senior professor is coming to inspect all the patients. The linens are changed; my face and body are washed. I am propped up in bed, cushioned by two pillows. The fevers are worse. The professor enters, followed by an entourage of doctors in white coats and nurses. He is a gray, slim man dressed in a smart suit, and he wears glasses. He parades from bed to bed as one of the younger doctors in a white coat talks before him. The professor asks a few questions, nods his head in a scholarly way, writes for a second on the board at the end of the bed, and then goes to the next patient. He is getting nearer to me and I feel quite anxious. He comes to me. The young doctor is nervous too. The pockets of his white coat bulge, full of pamphlets and papers, and he has his listening tube hung from his neck like a scarf. The young doctor starts to talk about me but is interrupted. 'Oh, here she is,' the professor says, and looks over his glasses at me. I try to smile. The professor continues in a voice that echoes his station in life, 'Yes, I have had calls about her . . . carry on,' he says to the junior doctor, who starts babbling in medical words. The professor listens and asks several questions of the young doctor that sound like a knife stabbing cheese. The young doctor is pouring sweat; it is as though he is being interrogated. 'Oh, terrible, terrible,' the professor says, slowly shaking his head. He then says in a voice that will be obeyed, 'I would give her maximum doses of the antibiotics . . . she is young. Her kidneys will be fine . . . what choice is there?'

He scribbles in the chart and is about to walk on when he halts and comes to stand next to my bed. He reaches his hand down and touches my arm. 'What is your name?' he asks in a kindly tone. 'Batuk,' I say. 'Batuk, that is a lovely name. Now, how are you feeling today?' 'Good . . . Professor . . . thank you,' I answer. 'Well, that is a good girl,' he says. 'I want you to do your best to get better.' He smiles at me, a large empty smile, takes his hand off my arm, and walks on to the next patient.

★   ★   ★

Even though there is a stack of paper next to my bed, I have not written for days. The policeman seems to have lost interest in my writing too. The times I am in high fever now exceed those in which I am cool. The bent-over old orderly somehow keeps up with my demand for dry towels to wipe my soaking head and body. When I reach my hand across to the little square wooden table that is next to my bed, there is always a dry towel there. The nurses check my temperature all the time but have stopped trying to make me drink the soup.

On top of the intense pain between my legs and the never-ceasing fevers, I start coughing. The trouble is, I am too weak to cough up the thick slime in my lungs. The nurse sits me forward, pounds on my back for a while, waits for me to spit up what looks like congealed yogurt, and off she goes. With each bout of fever, my strength, or what remains, is sapped a little more. I try so hard to cough. Last night I had a terrible incident — I coughed and coughed; some other patient told me to be quiet, but I could not. So I concentrated all my strength and did one huge cough. As the slime trickled out of my mouth I also did brown and pissed in the bed. I was too ashamed to tell anyone and lay in its warmth. The nurse scolded me only gently in the morning before she cleaned me.

The doctor today asked if I'd had TB. I told him I had it when I was little. 'I think it has come back,' said the doctor. 'Oh,' I said.

They have given me more pain medication with a needle, for which I thank them. The nurse cleans Bunny Rabbit and tries not to show emotion, but I can see white, smelly cream on the dressings. I look at my piss-bag and there is brown in that. I can also see that the skin of my thighs is bright red. The nurse cleans me up and waits. She is patient and the room is no longer that noisy. The orderly still delivers clean towels but I no longer have the strength to say thank you. I try to mouth to him. He pads my head with a cool towel and pushes a cold glass to my lips. As I sip, I taste sherbet. It is cool and sweet but a flood of warmth courses through my body like the river does in the monsoon, flooding her banks. The black ink starts to dissolve and I feel it seeping away from me. I am a child back on my father's lap. I smell perfumes and food and sweat on him. He pushes more sherbet in my mouth and I hear my tiny, naughty voice, 'Daddy, Daddy . . . please, please. Go on, tell me.' 'No,' he says like a wisp of breeze against my ear. But I know he will bend to my will. 'Daddy, please tell me my story.' Then, as his soft voice unfolds, his chest rumbles with each beloved syllable and I inhale not only him, but also the essence of the river that connects us all.

THE SILVER-EYED LEOPARD

In a land far away from here lived a queen. She was prized for her extraordinary beauty. But as beautiful as she was, she was also wise. She ruled her vast kingdom in peace and prosperity. No one in the kingdom went without food or shelter and no one could remember the last war. The queen was loved by all.

She had become queen at the age of nine after her mother and father died from the plague that had swept through the kingdom years before. Her parents had caught the plague as they had tended their sick subjects in the sanitarium on the outskirts of the city. They had fallen prey to the terrible illness together and died in each other's embrace, eternally bonded by their love of each other and for their people.

The nine-year-old child princess was appointed queen after seven weeks of mourning. Since the day of her enthronement, Gahil had been by her side as her devoted advisor. Gahil had been the king's sword bearer and there was no one in the kingdom the king had trusted more. The king had asked Gahil on his deathbed to be the child queen's guardian. He had made Gahil swear an oath to serve her always and to never let her leave the confines of the palace grounds for fear of her befalling the same fate that befell himself and his beloved queen. Gahil had fulfilled his oath from that day onward. From the day the crown had been placed on the nine-year-old princess's head, Gahil had loved the princess queen as if she were his own daughter. The princess queen had come to love Gahil as a father. Even as the queen entered adulthood and became a mighty, strong, and independent ruler, Gahil remained at her side. The queen never left the palace grounds and the chronicles recorded her name as the Queen of the Great Palace.

Every day the queen would attend to the affairs of state in the morning, and after her daily walk in the palace gardens she would lunch on bread, mango, and ass's milk. After the second chime, she would meet with her subjects, one and then another, resolving disputes and listening to requests. She received subjects late into the evening and often would ask her attendants to carry the aging Gahil to his chamber, as he would fall asleep from the length of his days.

The queen had completed twenty years of rule; the land prospered like never before and the people were at peace. One day, after many weeks of meditation, Gahil took the queen aside and said, 'Mighty queen and beloved ruler' (this is how he addressed his queen however many times she told him not to), 'may I please speak privately and frankly with you?' 'Of course, oh wisest of *all the wise' (this is how the queen addressed Gahil, even though he begged her not to). The queen was anticipating a long debate regarding a legal ruling she had made. Often, she would debate Gahil on matters of the law until deep into the night; she enjoyed pitting her razor-sharp mind against Gahil's gentle logic. They often disagreed, but how they loved to argue and joust in debate. However, on this occasion, Gahil's concern was not the law.*

He said, 'Your Majesty, you have ruled your land with wisdom and kindness for twenty years, and the people are at peace and the children are well fed. Have you thought of the future?' The queen knew exactly what Gahil was getting at but played ignorant. 'Wisest advisor, what is it you mean?' 'Your Majesty, have you considered marriage so that your kingdom may have an heir? Without an heir, the kingdom could become unstable. I beg of you, mighty and most beautiful of queens, please, at least consider taking suitors. My queen cannot age alone.' The queen laughed in response to Gahil's prodding. It was not the first time that the issue of her marriage had been raised. Secretly she agreed with Gahil. She knew her kingdom could only be secure with an heir apparent. Also, in secret, despite the love of Gahil and all her people, she was lonely for a companion. 'Learned and wisest master, what would you suggest? I was planning to grow old alongside you.' Gahil was ready for this opening. 'Your Majesty, let your government send forth a proclamation that their beloved queen will consider suitors for the sixty days after the third moon.' The queen thought, looked at her beloved Gahil, and said, 'Let it be so.'

The kingdom buzzed with gossip of the queen taking a suitor. 'Will it be the king of Bohemia?' one person asked. 'No, surely it will be the prince of Jerusalem,' said another. 'Rubbish,' said a third, 'it will be the royal prince of Persia.' The only thing that was clear was that no one could agree. It soon became the only topic people spoke of in the taverns and the village squares.

When the proclamation went forth across the far reaches of the earth that the legendary Queen of the Great Palace would consider suitors, hundreds of men arrived. They came on horses, in chariots, and on elephants. Every day more suitors rode into the city and the queen met with them all. One brought gold, another brought jewels; some brought furs and some brought magical silks. They all received the sincerest of thanks from the queen but none left with her hand in marriage. Gahil would say of one, 'He is a wonderful warrior,' but the queen would answer, 'But he has no appreciation for music — how could I marry such a man?' Gahil would say of another suitor, 'How beautiful are his features,' and the queen would answer, 'He is not skilled in mathematics — how will he help manage our grain stores?' And so it went on. Whenever Gahil found an attribute, his beloved queen would find a fault. Soon the sixty days would be up and Gahil realized he was fighting a losing battle. The queen, on the other hand, was irritated that so much time had been taken away from the affairs of state and her people by Gahil's scheme to find her a husband. But her loneliness started to grow within her. At first, this was a tiny seed of a feeling, but soon it became a forest of emptiness.

There was only one day left of the sixty-day proclamation and the queen (and even Gahil) looked forward to the return of normalcy. However, in the dead of night there rode into the city a prince. He rode on a horse that was so white and so glistening you could see the stars and the moon reflected in the sheen of its fur. The horse was magnificent but the prince who rode upon him more magnificent still. The prince was kept warm by a coat made from the furs of Russia. He wore a shirt and pants woven from the silk of China and boots cobbled from the leather of Turkey inlaid with pearl from Abyssinia. The man himself was tall and broad. He had eyes of ebony, hair of jet, and skin browned by the sun.

In the middle of the night, the prince began to pound on the outer gate to the palace. 'What is it?' the night guard called out. 'Tell your queen that the Prince of Princes is here to seek her hand in marriage.' 'Sire,' the guard replied, for he could see that this handsome man was a nobleman, 'I cannot admit you in the middle of the night, for the queen and her attendants are asleep. I would ask that you return in the morning to seek an audience.' 'Guard,' the prince responded, 'I must see the queen immediately, for I have a gift for her that is more precious than all eternity.' The guard was intrigued. 'Can I see this gift, sire?' The prince held up a small box of red wood, inlaid with gold and precious stones of many colors. 'Guard, it is in here. But I may show its contents only to the queen herself. No other person may see it,' said the prince. 'Sire, I must still ask that you return morning hence. I assure you that the queen will grant you an audience then.'

272

Gahil had been unable to sleep and was walking through the palace grounds in the dead of night. He was troubled. He was getting old and knew that soon he would die and there would be no one left to care for his queen. He heard the commotion at the palace gate and listened in the shadows. The words of the prince impressed him but if the truth were told, he was growing desperate to see his queen wed. He stepped from the shadows before the guard. The guard bowed. 'Lord Chancellor,' he said, calling Gahil by his official title, 'this prince wishes to see our queen immediately.' The prince turned to the elderly man from whom every breath was wisdom and said, 'Honored Lord Chancellor, I am the Prince of Princes and I have come to seek the queen's hand. I have a gift for her drawn from the heavens' — he held up the jeweled box — 'but I must give it to Her Majesty immediately.' Gahil was about to deny the prince his request and suggest that he return in the morning just as the guard had done, but the elderly advisor had the power of inner sight. The Lord Chancellor stared into the depth of the prince's soul and all he saw there was beauty. Gahil used his magical powers, mastered through years of meditation and learning, to look in the crevices and corners of the prince's heart, and all he saw there was purity. Gahil said, to the astonishment of the guard, 'Come into the palace, Prince of Princes. I will inquire of the queen whether she will give you an audience at this extraordinary hour.'

The prince and his horse entered the palace confines behind the slow, stooping gait of the old advisor. Gahil awoke messengers and sent them to the queen's chamber to ask whether she would take an audience for an urgent matter of state. The queen was gently awakened by her lady-in-waiting, who had served her from childhood. The lady-in-waiting was almost as old as Gahil, whom she had secretly loved all of her life. 'My queen,' her lady said in a gentle whisper, 'the Lord Chancellor seeks an urgent audience with you.' In all her reign the queen had never been awakened by Gahil even once in the middle of the night and so she knew that this must be a matter of the utmost urgency.

The queen put on a simple gown of raw white cotton and ran barefoot, with haste, to the audience chamber. She feared a catastrophe in her kingdom or that her beloved Gahil had fallen ill. As she entered the chamber, the queen said, panting, 'Beloved wise of the wise, what brings your call for an audience with me in the dead of night?' Gahil replied, eyes downcast, 'The queen of my heart, I beg your forgiveness, but please, I beg of you, give audience to the Prince of Princes who has come to see you urgently.'

Out of the corner of the room stepped the Prince of Princes, bearing the red wooden box. He bowed to the queen, who even without her jewels and finery was the most beautiful woman he had ever seen. 'What is this?' the queen asked of Gahil. 'The Prince of Princes has come to seek your hand,' Gahil answered in his slow, gentle voice. The queen's wisdom became veiled by a sheet of anger. 'What . . . in the dead of night, I am called from my chamber to see another suitor . . . Chancellor Gahil, I am so angered by this foolishness.' The old man fell to the floor. 'Oh Queen of Queens, I would rather be thrown into a pit of fire than anger you. I beg you to forgive me.' The queen rushed to the old man and helped him to his feet. 'You foolish old man,' she said, and kissed him lightly on the cheek, 'this prince of yours must be special indeed that you would awaken your queen for him.' 'Oh my queen,' Gahil responded, 'he is.' The queen turned her attention to the prince standing before her. 'Oh prince from distant lands, what I pray brings you to my palace so late in the night and what cannot wait that you keep my learned chancellor from his bed?'

The Prince of Princes looked upon the Queen of Queens and loved her with all his heart. So too the queen looked upon the prince and loved him in return. She however remained veiled by anger and by the fear of opening her heart to another. 'Oh queen,' the prince said, 'I have a gift for you that you must receive immediately, for it cannot wait. May I so beg your indulgence?' His voice possessed its own music. 'So what gift do you bring me, oh prince, that could not wait until the morning?' said the queen with a voice that was falsely aloof and irritated (old Gahil chuckled to himself, since he had never heard his queen speak in this way and so he knew that she was in love — at last).

The prince brought his dark eyes upon the radiant queen and found he could hardly speak. This is how people who are in love behave. The prince spoke timidly. 'I have a gift for her most beautiful and wise Majesty.' He opened the box and took from it a beautiful clear rock the size of a fist. The prince put the box on the floor and held out the rock in the palm of his hand for the queen to see. Was it a diamond? If

276

so, it would be the largest in the world. The queen stepped closer to see. As she did, a drop of water fell from the prince's hand to the floor. Then another drop fell and then another. 'Ice,' shouted the queen. 'You woke me up to see a piece of ice! My scientists have cooled my chamber with pieces of ice a thousand times larger than that.' Cloaked in her anger, she turned to the Lord Chancellor and shouted, 'This is it! No more suitors,' and with that, she ran from the chamber.

The prince remained standing exactly where he had been, the piece of ice gradually melting from his hand and forming a little pool of water beneath it. Gahil watched for a while but then left the chamber in sadness. He bade the guard show the prince out when he was ready to leave.

The queen returned to her chamber furious and explained to her lady-in-waiting what had transpired. The old servant listened and understood — her wisdom was even greater than Gahil's and far more carefully hidden. The lady-in-waiting waited for the queen's anger to lessen and then spoke quietly as the queen paced in her chamber. 'Does my queen require a drink of water to calm her nerves?' 'Thank you,' answered the queen, 'I would love some water.' The lady-in-waiting then took a glass and went to the queen's private chamber and filled the glass with diamonds from one of the queen's treasure chests. She then handed this to the queen. 'What is this?' the queen asked, puzzled. 'My queen, it is your water,' answered the elderly servant. The queen wrongly assumed that her lady-in-waiting was confused because of the late hour. The queen said, 'I cannot drink diamonds.'

At that moment the blinding veil of anger lifted from the queen and in a moment she realized her mistake. The Prince of Princes' gift to her was not the block of ice but himself. It was the warmth of his heart and the steadiness of his hand that he offered the queen, not another diamond. She stared at the cup of worthless diamonds in her hand under the caring gaze of her lady-in-waiting. A single drop of love is a gift of more value than all the jewels on earth. The queen was immediately aware that she loved the Prince of Princes with all of her heart. She fled from her chamber to find her prince, and as she did so a tear of happiness fell from the eye of her lady-in-waiting to the floor.

The queen raced to the audience chamber and threw open the door. The prince was not there. There was simply a pool of water in the middle of the floor. The queen ran from the chamber to the palace gates, which she had never left in all her life. When she reached the gate, hardly able to breathe, the guard bowed, for he had never seen his queen up close and certainly never barefoot, dressed in a simple cotton robe. The queen could not catch her breath. 'Where is the prince?' she gasped. The guard answered, 'He rode from here a few minutes ago . . . you can still hear the horse hooves.' In the deep silence of the night he was right, but the sound was disappearing.

The queen ran back to the audience room and threw herself over the little pool of water. She desperately tried to drink the water, licking it from the floor like a thirsty nomad when he finds water in the desert. Tears filled her eyes as the prince's love touched her lips and was swallowed inside of her. A veil of anger will lift, but love is forever blinding.

The queen ran to the palace stables. The stable boy lay asleep as usual in the loft. He could not believe it when he saw the queen before him. One of the royal horses was already saddled and she leaped upon the horse and galloped at full speed through the open palace gates as the guard watched, astounded. Everyone knew the queen had never left the palace in her whole life.

The queen rode in the direction from which she had heard the hoof sounds. She rode all through the night but never saw the Prince of Princes or heard the echo of his horse. She was in despair.

As the sun rose, her horse was tiring and slowed. She brought it to a gentle walk. She had never seen her kingdom before; she had never seen the fields that every year filled the grain stores or the houses that her people lived in, and she had never seen children playing in the early morning sun. All of a sudden a glistening caught her eye. In the distance she saw another pool of her prince's love melted onto the grass. She drove her horse at full gallop to the lake. When she reached it she saw a lake of her prince's love stretched before her as far as her eye could see. Remember, the queen had never seen a natural lake before, since she had never left her palace. She leaped from the horse and ran into the pool of love.

The queen had not only never seen a lake before but had never been taught to swim. And so, the Queen of Queens drowned. She did not cry out because she understood that this was how it felt to be consumed by love.

The only creature on earth that saw what

happened next was the royal horse, who was unable to tell a soul. As the Queen of Queens disappeared beneath the water, out from the water walked a white leopard. It was a beautiful, lean, muscular creature with a coat that glistened so that you could see the stars and the moon reflected in the sheen of her fur. The leopard had eyes of silver, for it carried the soul of the Queen of all Queens.

The leopard then ran with a gentle stride across the borders of Kumara into the eastern lands. She ran through rains and snows, across the plains of Abyssinia, and into the mountains of the Himalaya. The leopard climbed along long-forgotten passes and across rock faces that no one even knew existed.

After many moons she chanced upon a cave. There, within it, seated in lotus pose, was the Prince of Princes. He was naked and alone. The leopard looked upon the Prince of Princes through her eyes of silver. Through him she saw heaven and earth melt into one beautiful river of love. In his eyes, the circles of love spun over earth, connecting a crying child to a beggar laughing, connecting a thrust of hope to a cry of despair, resolving evil with the good. Everything else is illusion. The silver-eyed leopard then sat at the feet of the *Prince of Princes* for eternity.

Writing my story has exhausted me. I concentrate in my flickering consciousness to look over the hat vendor's shoulder and see his face. I cannot, but I am near.

The following is the text from a piece of paper folded in half and inserted into the blue notebook

<u>Handwritten in pencil</u>.

A Hat's Tale
Everything is foretold,
Yet in all we have choice.
Our good deeds sit upon a scale:
Tilt it this way and the sun rises, Tilt it
    that and all that remains of the flame
    is a spiral of smoke.

Everything is given,
Yet upon us all floats a veil.
The vendor happily extends you credit.
But, as you borrow, he shall write it down.

Every night the collector makes his rounds
And takes from you asleep precisely what
is his.
For your debt is inscribed
And your judgment, truth.

We do hope that you have enjoyed reading this large print book.

Did you know that all of our titles are available for purchase?

We publish a wide range of high quality large print books including:
Romances, Mysteries, Classics
General Fiction
Non Fiction and Westerns

Special interest titles available in large print are:
The Little Oxford Dictionary
Music Book
Song Book
Hymn Book
Service Book

Also available from us courtesy of Oxford University Press:
Young Readers' Dictionary
(large print edition)
Young Readers' Thesaurus
(large print edition)

For further information or a free brochure, please contact us at:
Ulverscroft Large Print Books Ltd.,
The Green, Bradgate Road, Anstey,
Leicester, LE7 7FU, England.
Tel: (00 44) 0116 236 4325
Fax: (00 44) 0116 234 0205

TRUE MURDER

Yaba Badoe

Eleven-year-old Ajuba has been abandoned at a Devon boarding school by her Ghanaian father. Haunted by the circumstances of her mother's breakdown and her life in Ghana, she falls under the spell of new girl Polly Venus and her family. But all is not what it seems in the Venus household and Ajuba can only watch as the family tear itself apart. One day the girls find the bones of a dead baby wrapped up in an old coat in the attic of the Venus manor house. Obsessed with the detectives of the American magazine serial *True Murder*, the girls set out to find out what happened to the baby and as the summer draws to a close, three tragedies conflate, with catastrophic results.

LEFTOVERS

Laura Wiess

Forgiveness is far off for teenagers Blair and Ardith, best friends and accomplices in a terrible crime. At the home of the only adult they trust, a police officer, the girls confess every horrifying detail. But it becomes clear the act wasn't out of malice or revenge, but born of fierce loyalty and unimaginable desperation. Written off by abusive parents and mocked and shunned by their classmates, Blair and Ardith had found a safe haven with one another. And when that haven was threatened, they knew they must do everything in their power to protect it. Whatever the cost.